SURVIVAL

Library Pet, Book 2

JG JEROME

SURVIVAL
LIBRARY PET, BOOK 2

By JG Jerome
Cover by Albert Chauw
Edited by Heather Jerome

"Love is at the root of everything. Love or the lack of it."

— FRED ROGERS

FOREWORD

This is an adult fantasy for mature folks that comes out of my twisted mind. They are my dreams, daydreams, and fantasies transcribed onto paper.

As such, this story is explicit. It includes descriptions of genitalia, descriptions of sexual activities, mild BDSM, erotic rope arts, martial arts, violence, and probably many other things that might possibly offend someone in our judgemental society.

I also write in a first person, slice-of-life style.

If you are offended or disgruntled by any of those things, then kindly close the book, tell Amazon you made a mistake, get your refund, and go forth to enjoy life elsewhere. I wish you the best.

If you're not dissuaded, then welcome to 'Survival.'

As a gentle reminder, in book 1, 'Surrender,' Marcus and Denise met, and an immediate attraction caused them to fall from one intense afternoon of passion into a deeply emotional relationship that was threatened by Denise's ex-husband, Daniel Connolly. Daniel's attack caught both Marcus and Denise by surprise, and Daniel died at Marcus' hand. Now as their connection strengthens, Marcus and Denise must turn their focus to surviving the aftermath of that fateful night.

PROLOGUE

Denise reminisces as she stands where Marc first found her adjusting her breasts because her bra was pinching. *'I never thought I would be grateful for an underwire.'*

Denise sighs with a bright smile and goes to ask someone at the desk where the meeting room is. With directions in hand, she threads her way through the stacks to find the room where she is meeting her best friend, Aliyah.

Aliyah Sadduzai is a reporter for the Topcka Capital Journal, and Denise chuckles as she thinks about how Aliyah seems to prefer to work from the library or one of the two coffee shops within walking distance of the newspaper's office. Aliyah was so proud to get the internship at the newspaper. She couldn't stop talking about the excitement of the newsroom. Her fascination with the newsroom continued through her first year as a full-time reporter. Slowly, she started spending more time at Juli's Coffee Bean or the library and less time in the newsroom.

Denise finds the small conference room and sees the gorgeous Pakistani woman typing on her laptop. Denise has always been amazed that Aliyah doesn't have a pack of men following her. She has a beautiful, exotic, lightly tanned face highlighted by slightly plump lips and eyes like dark pools. Despite habitually having a scarf wrapped around her head and shoulders in the traditional hijab of Pakistan, her luxurious hair has a mind of its own and peaks out to tease the eye. Aliyah always wears loose, conservative, long skirts or slacks with long tunics or conservative blouses to honor the modesty her faith espouses. However, Aliyah's garment choices don't hide her perfect size six figure. Then again, Denise has often seen Aliyah in her preferred attire of yoga pants and soft sweaters or cotton camisole tank tops when she's at home - just like Denise herself.

Today, Aliyah is wearing a cream colored brocade hijab over a light blue tunic and dark, ankle-length skirt.

Denise grins at her BFF thinking she's the most beautiful woman she's ever met.

Aliyah looks up and smiles brightly. "Denise!" Aliyah exclaims as she launches around the small conference table to wrap her arms around Denise.

Denise kisses her friend's cheek and thinks, *'That's nearly as nice as when Marc does it.'*

Aliyah looks at Denise worriedly without releasing the full body press. "I'm sorry to drag you through this, Denise. My editor is going crazy, and all the news stations are clambering for any little tidbit about what happened."

Denise squeezes Aliyah closely before releasing her and setting down her satchel on the table to take off her light trench coat. Denise says, "I don't mind telling you the story, Allie. Especially if it will help you at work."

Aliyah shrugs with a self-deprecating smile. "I do pretty well at work despite all the grumbling about the 'raghead bitch' when I get a front page or a good story," she says.

"If you ever decide to do something about it, I know an excellent equal rights and sexual harassment lawyer," Denise says as she takes a seat.

Aliyah takes a seat and shuts her laptop before she pulls out a recorder and notepad. She's about to ask a question when Denise interrupts her. "Aliyah, I need you to keep my boyfriend out of this. No mention of his name, nor where he lives or what he does. I want to keep him an enigma. I'm not convinced that Daniel's family won't try for some kind of retribution - attack Marc as some kind of payback."

Aliyah nods, "So, his name is Marc, and he shall not be mentioned again other than as 'the boyfriend.' My editor will of course tell me to put it in the story, so I will have to claim ignorance. I will perhaps ask you on tape about his name, and you can state exactly what you just told me."

Denise nods. "Yes. That should work nicely."

Aliyah says, "I have wanted to expose the Connolly family ever since I heard them bragging at your wedding. I could never get permission to go to Salina to investigate. Now one of them makes a mess in my town. Shall we begin?"

"Okay," Denise agrees.

Aliyah turns on her recorder and begins talking, "I am Aliyah Sadduzai, reporter for the Topeka Capital-Journal, interviewing Denise Schneider at the Topeka Public Library on October fourth, two o'clock PM." Then she turns her attention to her notes before asking a question.

"Denise, you are the Law Clerk for the Chief Justice of the Kansas Supreme Court and a practicing lawyer for nearly six years. Is that correct?"

"Yes."

Aliyah continues, "I understand you were attacked by Police Officer Daniel Connolly in your home the evening of October first. Would you please tell me what happened?"

"Certainly, Miss Sadduzai. I was at my rented house in Topeka. My boyfriend and I had been packing out my house."

Aliyah interrupts, "What is your boyfriend's name, Ms. Schneider?" Aliyah winks and Denise almost giggles.

"I'm not going to tell you that, Miss Sadduzai. I'm afraid of reprisals from Daniel's family, and I would rather my boyfriend not be subjected to the craziness of the Connolly family. They have a reputation in my hometown of Salina for being vindictive." Aliyah smiles broadly at that tidbit and gives Denise a thumbs up gesture. "I will tell you only about his actions during that evening."

Denise pauses before continuing her narrative. "We had just finished dinner. We had ordered pizza and salads. We cleaned up. My boyfriend asked me to move in with him, and I agreed. We were celebrating our agreement when I heard a key slide into the door. I remember gasping 'Oh no' and grabbing my pepper spray from my purse. I had a restraining order against Daniel since he beat me the day I filed for divorce. It was overwhelming to hear him at my door."

Denise pulls a tissue from her satchel as her gaze gets distant. "I had been afraid of Daniel for a couple of years by that point. I changed the locks on the house and started carrying the pepper spray after that last beating. Anyway..." she sighs heavily. "...my boyfriend said 'Call 911,'" and he looked around the room like he was assessing a battlefield. I dialed 911 and got the pepper spray in the correct position to use. Daniel kept beating on the door and yelling for me to let him in. I explained to the 911 operator that my ex-husband was trying to break in and that he was a Topeka police officer. The dispatcher, a very polite and helpful gentleman, sent a unit to the house and waited on the line with me."

Denise starts to shred the tissue as she talks. "I heard an especially loud boom, and the door cracked above the lock. Daniel yelled 'Open the door, bitch!' I relayed to the operator that he was breaking the door. My boyfriend told me to get behind the kitchen counter. He ensured I was sitting in front of the dishwasher, turned out the lights, and he disappeared. Daniel yelled 'You can't hide,' and started shooting through the door. I don't recall how many shots it was, but it was enough for Daniel to kick the solid wood door and have the lock break out of it. The bullets damaged the cabinet I was hiding behind. Daniel yelled out 'Honey, I'm home' and then the door cracked loudly. It sounded like the door thudded twice in quick succession. Then there were sounds of a scuffle. Then my boyfriend turned on the lights and held me. He said Daniel was 'out cold.' We held each other until the police arrived. I think we only waited about a minute after that. The paramedics followed shortly thereafter. They tried to resuscitate Daniel, but he died on the floor."

Aliyah asks, "How did your boyfriend overpower an armed criminal?"

Denise says, "I'm not sure whether to say 'sadly' or 'fortunately,' but he is a veteran. He served in Afghanistan, and based on some of the stories he told me, this was just a minor inconvenience to him. He was so angry that someone would attack me. I didn't see any of the actual altercation, but I heard him tell the police that he took the closet pole out of the coat closet and used it to disarm Daniel. Daniel tried to pull another weapon, so my boyfriend hit him in the throat with the closet pole. Daniel fell backward, and his head hit before the rest of his body, severely fracturing his skull. That's what caused his death."

"How did you and Daniel meet?" Aliyah asks, trying to build some background.

Denise sighs. "It's like a Hollywood romance gone bad. Daniel was a year ahead of me in high school. We started dating halfway through my freshman year - the stereotypical cheerleader and football captain romance. After he graduated, he went to Butler County Community College for a semester before going to the police academy in Hutchinson so he could join the force in Salina. I graduated high school and started at Washburn. We continued to see each other regularly. Daniel transferred to the Topeka police department my sophomore year. I finished my degree and started law school. We were married a week after I graduated. I joined the Montblanc law firm, passed the bar, and started work as a lawyer. Our marriage was not great, but I kept working at it. I thought Daniel was too, despite the occasional shouting matches that more and more frequently ended up in me getting slapped. About nine months ago, I discovered that Daniel had been having an affair with a work colleague, so I filed for divorce. He beat me severely with his fists, and I ended up in the hospital. I stayed with my best friend and got the restraining order. It has been nearly five months since the divorce recorded, and I met my boyfriend shortly after the divorce was final."

"What kind of person was Daniel?" she asked.

Denise chuckles evilly. "Personally, I think he was a sonofabitch, but I didn't learn that until we were married. He could be very charming and very persuasive. I learned after I filed for divorce that he had been cheating on me as long as I knew him. High school class-mates, college classmates, his colleagues in the police department. He had several women strung along at any one time. I was so ashamed when I learned about them. I'm reasonably attractive. Why wasn't I enough? I figure that for him the conquest was the thrill. He was extremely possessive, too. He would get mad at me for spending time with my female friends and would fly into a rage if I spoke more than a casual greeting to a man. I should have never married him, but no one tells you this kind of stuff beforehand - only after. My best friend is the only person that ever spoke against him before I married him, but she's fearless and loves me dearly."

Aliyah reaches for Denise's hand as she looks at her questions.

"Ms. Schneider, are there any charges pending for either yourself or your boyfriend? Essentially, your boyfriend killed a police officer in uniform," Aliyah says.

Denise shakes her head decisively. "No. The investigating officers and a subsequent review both declared that M...my boyfriend was acting in self-defense. Additionally, they concluded that Daniel was acting in a criminal manner. The Topeka police are not very forgiving when one of their own doesn't meet their standards of conduct."

Aliyah says, "What did you mean by the Connolly family having a reputation for being vindictive?"

"As an attorney, I can tell you that most of what I know would only qualify as 'hearsay' in a court of law. After my divorce, several acquaintances that moved away from Salina reached out to me. They told me stories of extortion, reprisals, and missing persons that had stood up to the Connollys. The father of the family is the Chief of Police in Salina, and two of Daniel's three brothers are also on the Salina police force. The third is an officer in Hays. Joseph was a bully in school, but I never really knew Sean other than seeing him around town. I only met Michael at my wedding. Several Connolly cousins work in law enforcement across the state. People in Salina are afraid of the police. My parents moved to Tucson when I went to Washburn, but they refused to talk about the Connolly family for fear of reprisals, even in Arizona. My mom did say that she felt bad for the police chief's wife. Their daughter is a sweetheart; I just hope they don't destroy her."

Aliyah smiles, shuts off the recorder, and puts her pen down. She says, "Well, I can turn this into a good story. Thank you so much, Denise."

"It's my pleasure, Allie. You've helped me so much by listening to me over the years. Thank you," Denise pours out heartfelt gratitude.

Aliyah says, "So tell me about the 'amazing Marc.' You've been all aflutter since you met him."

"I can't help it, Allie! He's so kind, so attentive, and..." Denise looks to ensure the door is closed. "...he does things to my body that I couldn't even imagine. I never knew sex could be like this. I have literally passed out from pleasure from his loving ministrations. I've never felt so loved! I love him so much!"

Aliyah squirms uncomfortably in her chair. "Uh...that is nice. I am so happy for you. So, where are you living?"

"On a farm outside of Carbondale," she replies. "He's buying it from his father. His mother and brother are both dead. His father is in a nursing home with dementia and Alzheimers. He's fading, but not gone. I've enjoyed visiting with him. His name is Carl Hough."

Aliyah's eyes are inscrutable. "I'm very happy for you, Denise."

Denise squeezes the hand that Aliyah is still holding. "I need to get moving. We are going to Kansas City for the weekend. We're going to the Nelson, the theater, and I expect lots of fucking and lounging at the Fontaine. I can hardly wait."

Denise gets up and pulls on her trench. She tosses the shredded tissue in the bin and puts the strap for her satchel over her shoulder. She doesn't catch Aliyah's first expression - eyes narrowed and lips pursed in jealousy. Denise turns to catch a dreamy expression on Aliyah's face.

The two ladies hug, and Denise leaves the room and hurries to her SUV. As Denise sets her satchel on the seat, she realizes she has seen that expression frequently on her friend's face before but had always written it off as Aliyah's 'thinking face.' This time Denise is struck by how similar it is to the expression she has seen in her mirror as she thinks about Marcus - desire.

Denise thinks to herself, '*I must be imagining that.*'

ALIYAH IS NEARLY IN TEARS FROM FRUSTRATION AS DENISE disappears. She thinks, *'Why can't she love ME like that? I would love to take her off for a romantic getaway! It's my own fault. I keep letting my faith be an excuse. That and my fear because I really have no more idea how to love a woman than I do a man. I've never told her, so I can't blame her.'* She sighs heavily. *'Allah preserve me from my own foolishness, and please protect my Denise.'*

She packs her computer into her bag. *'I think the coffee shop will inspire me to write this well. Then I should go check into the office to irritate the bigots.'*

(06 OCT - SALINA, KANSAS - SEAN'S CONNOLLY'S DEN.)

"Did you read what that bitch in Topeka wrote about Daniel?" Sean Connolly growls.

"Yeah," his brother Joseph says. "She lacks the required respect for our family. It's been a frustrating few days."

Sean berates his younger brother, "Well if you hadn't sat on your ass so long, we might have gotten the name of Daniel's murderer before that bitch Denise got the record sealed."

Joseph waves a hand in an irritated dismissal. "Don't matter. We know it was her boyfriend. We'll find him. Then I'm gonna kill him slowly. I'm gonna butcher him while he's still alive."

Both brothers' faces light with fierce joy at the thought of dismembering the man that killed their little brother.

Joseph smirks as a thought takes root in his fevered brain. "The byline says Aliyah Sadduzai. That's gotta be foreign, and I think 'Aliyah' is a female name. How many foreign female reporters can there be in Topeka, Kansas?"

Sean grins. "Shouldn't be hard to find. Is that an Arabic name? Let's go teach this rag-head bitch some manners. We can look her up at our office to get an address from her driver's license. Maybe she knows the murderer's name. It's still early. We can finish this today."

❧ I ❧

WEEKEND IN KANSAS CITY

After the drama on Tuesday night, I thought Denise and I would have to cancel our planned trip to Kansas City for the weekend to have her possessions delivered, but we decided not to. I was able to get reservations at The Fontaine, a swank hotel at the Country Club Plaza. The Kansas City Repertory Theater unexpectedly extended their run of 'Cat on a Hot Tin Roof' through Saturday, and I was able to get seats for the show. Additionally, the Nelson Atkin Museum of Art had an exhibition called Under the Big Top that featured the Barnum and Bailey Circus, which we thought would be fun.

We packed reasonably fancy dress for the theater, casual clothes for during the day, and I packed an additional bag with some rope and toys for night time.

Denise got home about 3:30 Friday afternoon, and we headed off for Kansas City by four o'clock. We arrived about six despite Kansas City rush hour traffic.

That evening, we ate at the hotel restaurant and took a carriage ride through the Plaza before retiring to the hotel for love-making. We kept things pretty vanilla, but we did christen the bedroom, the bathroom counter, the sofa, and the entry hallway before we passed out.

Saturday, we broke our fast at the hotel and spent the rest of the morning and all afternoon at the Nelson Atkin Art Gallery. The 'Under the Big Top' exhibition was fascinating. Plus, the exhibit brought back good memories of going to the circus with my parents and brother as a kid. We lunched at the gallery and took in some of the other art on display throughout the afternoon.

When we returned to the hotel, I took Denise roughly over the arm of the sofa before we got ready for the evening show, 'Cat on a Hot Tin Roof' at KC Repertory Theater. We dressed up, and I swear I looked like a fourteen-year old kid walking around with a tent pole in my pants from how sexy and glamourous Denise looked in the gown she brought. I wore a tux. We were over-dressed compared to others at the theater, but not by much. I practiced tying Denise in a 'net dress' afterward, letting her ride the knots to bliss while I fucked her pretty mouth.

Sunday started with gentle wake-up sex followed by lazily reading the Kansas City and Topeka papers over brunch. The story on the lower half of the front page told a pretty damning story about Daniel Connolly. I swear, if the guy wasn't dead, the public would lynch him. Denise's friend Aliyah Sadduzai wrote the article, and she definitely communicated a dislike for Daniel and his family. She kept mostly to the facts; however, the way she used Denise's quotes set the tone masterfully. I'm a published writer, but Aliyah is leap years ahead of me in skill. I look forward to meeting her. I told Denise so.

Denise called Aliyah several times throughout brunch without any success in getting her friend to answer.

DENISE HANGS UP THE PHONE AGAIN AS WE PULL OFF OLD HIGHWAY 75 onto the dirt road that was named 117th Street sometime after I moved to Arizona. She says, "Aliyah still isn't answering her phone. I'm starting to worry about her."

"Why is that, Love?"

Denise looks off at the horizon. "You don't know the Connolly family, Marc. They are dreadful. I wish we had run by her place on the way back."

"We can run up there after we drop the bags off," I assure her. "Dad knows we were out of town this weekend - if his memory is functioning. It shouldn't be a problem to wait until tomorrow for a visit."

I turn south and we quickly approach the farm.

A blue Ford F350 pickup is parked on the road south of the yard facing north. I notice two figures seated in the front seat. I pull Denise's SUV into the driveway, and the pickup starts moving.

Something feels off. Rather than stopping for the mail, I continue down the driveway. The big pickup truck barrels across the yard on a vector to slam into us. I goose the powerful Infinity SUV to get out of the way, but they still manage to swerve and ram into the rear quarter-panel.

Two guys get out of the pickup. I get out and tell Denise, "Lock the door, and go get help!"

I grab my phone out of my pocket and key it to record before tossing it lightly into the grass.

The two guys look related to each other. They are big guys - like middle-aged high-school football players gone soft. Both have short, brush-cut hairstyles. One has a K-State ball cap on. The other is sporting a Hooters cap.. The older one, 'Hooters,' has some salt-and-pepper in his sidewalls and a bit of a paunch, but it hasn't 'done-lopped' over his belt yet. The other one, 'K-State,' has a thick waist and looks drunk. He sways a little bit as he reaches into the back of the truck to pull out a sledgehammer. The elder one pulls out a long-handled spade-style shovel as I hear Denise engage the locks.

The younger one says, "How did a pipsqueak like you manage to kill my brother?"

'Oh, shit,' is the first thought that comes to mind as Denise gets behind the driver's seat and pulls out. She drives through the back yard and disappears. I hear the engine rev as she heads north on the road until I see her drive past.

I think, '*Well at least I know who they are.*' I'm a little offended by the 'pipsqueak' comment. I am 6'3", 200 pounds, with broad shoulders.

Granted I still have a lean soldier's build, so they probably have me on body mass. I'm pretty certain I can handle these to jackasses since I don't see any firearms.

I figure I might as well wind them up to see if I can get them to do something stupid. "Well, your dumbass brother started shooting through the door, so I had to try to stop him. Apparently, he was too much of a pussy to survive."

The elder guy says, "Boy, you need to learn some respect for your betters."

I chuckle, "When I meet someone better than me, I do show respect. There are quite a few. Fortunately, neither of you two douchebags qualify."

The younger one blubbers, "My brother was a better man than three of you put together. You musta jumped him when he wasn't looking."

I nod, "That's exactly what I did. The dumbass shot around the lock, kicked in the door, and barrelled into the house. I kicked the door back at him and hit him with a closet pole. Then he was dead."

The elder one says, "We're going to beat you until all your bones are broken, boy."

The younger one bounces the sledgehammer against his palm. "Yeah. Then we're gonna butcher you like a hog. The last time I did that, the guy stayed alive for about an hour once I started cuttin' on him. Then we gave his meat to his family." He launches toward me and thrusts the head of the hammer at my torso. I slide to my right and flick a finger at his eye while stepping up the circle to catch the other guy swinging the shovel at me. I get both hands on the shovel and pull, which puts the stunned younger guy's face at the point of impact for the shovel.

The elder guy releases the shovel handle to catch himself as he falls to the ground. I use the shovel like a bo-staff and thrust the handle into the younger guy's crotch. I reverse it into the back of his head, and the guy crumples to the ground.

I notice the Hooters guy has a heavy revolver holstered behind his back with a matching leather cuff holster. He reaches for the weapon and gets it out of the holster as he rolls on the ground, but I'm in a good position. Since I swang the shovel through the younger guy's head, it is already on a downward arc.

I launch toward the older guy as he rolls to his back and tries to bring the gun to bear. Just before he gets the pistol pointed at me, the head of the shovel makes contact with his wrist. The weapon fires upon impact, and I hear a plink as the bullet hits the metal of the truck and ricochets past my head. The impact of the hard steel shovel on his wrist causes the guy to release the gun, dropping it on the grass. Fortunately, he reaches for the gun rather than dealing with me, giving me time to smack the guy in the back of the head with the flat of the shovel. I smack him twice before he gives up reaching for the gun to cover his head. I step around his head and turn the shovel on edge, swingng the blade of the shovel into his right forearm with an audible crunch. The dumbass rolls over on top of his arm to protect it, so I hit the back of his skull with the flat of the shovel again. The tough bastard finally collapses. I pick the revolver up by the barrel and place it on the hood of the truck.

I see the 'K-State' guy has the same kind of rig at the small of his back. I kneel down with a knee on his tailbone and pull an automatic from the holster and toss it behind me in the grass. I pull the cuffs off the guy, and secure his wrists. I pick up the pistol from the grass and set it on the hood of the truck beside the other one.

I kneel on the tailbone of the elder guy, and he starts to stir. I grab his right arm and pull it behind his back. He screams as the ends of the broken bones in his forearms grind against each other. He flinches, but I get the cuff on his wrist. I pin the broken arm to his back with my knee.

I tell him, "You can give me the other wrist, or I can keep fucking with the broken one until you pass out from the pain. Choose."

He rocks from side to side, and eventually the left arm finally appears.

"Palm up," I tell him. He rotates his palm, and I guide the elbow behind his back until I can snape the other cuff over his left wrist. He whines. I tell him, "Relax. If you stay still, I won't hurt you."

I check his ankles and find another holster with a small .32 caliber automatic. I pull the holster off and set it next to the first pistol. Sure enough, K-State has one, too. He tries to kick me as I pull it off, but I manage it by driving a knuckle punch into his calf. I pull his ankle holster and weapon off and place them next to the others as K-State yells at me. "I'm gonna kill you, mother-fucker."

I look down at him. "Oh? Maybe I should kill you now, rather than giving you a chance, dumbass. Castle Doctrine applies in this case."

"I'm a cop. You are in so much shit, mother-fucker. You can't do this to a cop," he yells.

Hooters barks, "Shut up, Joseph."

"Are you with the Carbondale police? The Osage County Sheriff maybe?" I ask.

"Fuck that. I'm with a real police department," he scoffs.

"Oh, so you're from Topeka? Lawrence? Kansas City?" I ask.

"Hell no. Salina!" he exclaims.

"Hmmm. I guess you're well out of your jurisdiction. Is beating and butchering people a standard practice in Salina?" I ask.

"Damned straight, mother-fucker," he growls.

"Hmmm. That should clear up some missing person cases," I ponder out loud.

Hooters yells, "Damnit, Joseph! Shut the fuck up!"

Joseph, AKA K-State, mutters, "I ain't saying nothing."

"Just relax," I tell him. "We'll have someone here to pick you up shortly. Your buddy needs to go to the hospital."

"Brother," he mutters. "My brother, Sean."

I chuckle as I pick up my phone and jump to the home screen before calling Denise.

"*Marc!*" she exclaims. "*Are you okay? The police are on their way!*"

"I'm fine, sweetheart. One of them is drunk, and they are both cuffed," I assure her.

"*Joseph is probably the drunk one,*" she responds.

"Uh....yeah. How did you know that?" I ask.

"*They are Daniel's brothers. Sean was already on the police force in Salina when I was a freshman in high school. Joseph was a senior, and Daniel was a sophomore,*" she says.

"They did accuse me of killing their brother. You coming home?" I ask.

"*I'll be right there,*" she says. "*I'm at the big farmhouse up the road.*"

Three minutes later, Denise shows up. She jumps out of the SUV and hugs me fiercely.

I murmur into my beautiful lady's ear. "Are you okay, Pet?" I hear sirens in the distance.

"Yes, Sir," she whimpers. "I've been so worried about you."

"I know, Love. Getting you away let me do what I needed to do. I'm glad you were safe," I tell her as I caress her back and her fabulous ass. I step back and look into her eyes. "Honey, would you call 911 and let them know to inform the responding officers that the attackers have been apprehended. They will be less likely to draw weapons when they arrive. Tell them we'll be leaning against the back of the SUV."

Denise kisses my hands and retrieves her phone. She calls 911 and gives them an update. I guide her to the back of the SUV and pull her into a hug as she talks to them. The sirens are getting louder, and I hear their engines roar as they get closer and closer. The sirens cut off as two Sheriff's Deputy cars speed past our property. The one in the back slams on the brakes and slides into my mailbox. The one in front slams on its breaks immediately thereafter, and they both back up and pull into the driveway.

I put my hands on top of my head. Denise kisses me and walks over to the cars.

I can see the deputies are entranced by my beautiful girlfriend. I bet she's fighting the urge to tell them 'hey, my eyes are up here.'

I call out, "All good, Denise?"

"Yes, Marcus." She smiles over her shoulder and winks at me before turning her charm on the deputies.

Another deputy in a car, followed by a pickup, each with the Sheriff's Office logo, slow and pull into the driveway.

The Sheriff and the new deputy join the circle with Denise. Denise explains the situation to the circle of officers.

"My name is Denise Schneider. I am the Law Clerk for the Chief Justice of the Kansas Supreme Court. My boyfriend and I, Marcus Hough, were returning from Kansas City after a weekend out of town.

As we approached the driveway, we saw this truck sitting beside the road. As we turned in the driveway, the truck started moving. They drove across the lawn, and I thought they were going to ram us. Marcus managed to accelerate, so they were only able to clip the back of the car, but it spun us around. Fortunately, we weren't close to the propane tank."

Denise takes a deep breath, and I smile at the effect that has on all four men. She continues, "Marcus got out of the truck and told me to lock it and get away to get help. I locked the door after he was out, crawled across the console, and started the car up. I drove around the east side of the house across the yard, out to the road, and turned north toward high ground. The 911 operator picked up before I got to the neighbor's driveway, so I pulled in there and told her what happened. Shortly thereafter, I got a call from Marcus, so I hung up with the operator to take his call. He told me that he had them in cuffs, so I came back here. I called the 911 operator again to tell her Marus had apprehended the attackers. Then you all showed up and wiped out the mailbox."

The deputy has the grace to look embarrassed. "Sorry, about that ma'am. I'll fix it for you."

The sheriff, a tall, athletic man, with dark hair and a chronic five o'clock shadow, walks over to join me with one of the deputies.

The sheriff introduces himself, "Hi. I'm Sheriff Michael Eskola. Who are you?"

I extend my hand. "Marcus Hough, Sheriff. It's a pleasure to meet you. Wish it were under different circumstances."

"I'm sure. Why do you think it's a pleasure, Mr. Hough?" he asks with a piercing stare.

I chuckle. "I normally vote for more candidates from the other party. I liked your messaging better than the other guy's, and you've got a good record. It's a pleasure to see the guy I voted for on the job."

He smiles mildly, but it doesn't quite reach his eyes. "Well thank you, Mr. Hough. What happened here?

I shrug, "We saw them when we were approaching the house. They cut across the yard and tried to ram us. You can see the tracks in the grass. They were aimed right at the passenger compartment, but luckily I was able to get far enough ahead of them that they only impacted the rear quarter panel. I got out of the truck and turned the recorder on my phone as they were pulling a sledgehammer and a shovel out of the back of their truck. Denise drove off, and I dropped my phone in the grass. They attacked me, and I defended myself. I knocked out the younger one, I think his name is Joseph Connolly. He was trying to hit me with the sledgehammer. He also acted inebriated. The elder one, I think his name is Sean Connolly, tried to hit me with a shovel before he pulled a gun. I broke his arm with the shovel and disarmed him. He got a shot off, but he missed. I felt it ricochet pass my head. I put his own cuffs on him, and then I cuffed Joseph with his. I found ankle holsters on both of them. All the weapons are on the hood of their truck. Then I called Denise, and she came back."

"Do you know why they attacked you?" he asks.

I nod, "As they got out of the truck, they accused me of killing their brother. That's when they grabbed the weapons...er...tools. I think what he actually said was 'How did a pipsqueak like you manage to kill my brother?' That was the younger one. The older one said they were going to break all my bones, and then the younger one said he was going to butcher me like a hog after that. He said he'd done it before. They claimed to be police officers from Salina, Kansas."

"You have a recording of this?" the sheriff asks.

I shrug. "I think so. I haven't checked it yet."

I pull out the phone and find the open window for the recorder. Apparently, it's still running, so I stop the recording and save it. I save it to my DropBox and transfer a copy to the sheriff's phone via near-field communications or NFC.

Denise approaches as the files transfer. She says, "Sheriff, both of these men are known to me. The Connolly family has run law enforcement in Salina for years." The file finished transferring, so I turned the recorder back on and held the microphone toward the conversation. Denise continues, "I was married to their younger brother, and we were recently divorced. My ex-husband, Daniel Connolly, tried to break into my house in Topeka this past Tuesday night by shooting through my door. He threatened my life, and I believe he would have killed me because he had beaten me severely when we were married. I had a restraining order on him. Daniel forced the door open, and Marcus defended me."

"I hit him repeatedly with a closet pole," I tell him. "Denise's ex didn't survive. Denise moved in with me on Wednesday."

Denise says, "I managed to get a court order to seal the record by Thursday morning. It's unlikely they got our location from the Topeka police. I don't know how they knew to look here."

Joseph yells, "Think you're so smart, bitch?" I turn the phone toward him. "That rag-head reporter didn't hold out long once we started beating on her."

Sean whispers, "Joseph! Shut the fuck up!"

Denise gasps before she explains to the sheriff, "Aliyah. Aliyah Sadduzai is the reporter with the Topeka Capital-Journal that interviewed me for the story in this morning's paper. She's a friend, and she hasn't been answering her phone all day."

"Do you know her address?" the sheriff asks.

Denise nods and pulls up her phone and looks it up. She shows it to the sheriff. He takes it and walks over to his truck. I see him talking into a handset, and I hear something intelligible respond from the speaker in his pickup.

Denise hugs me close. She murmurs, "I hope she's alright."

While we're waiting on the Sheriff's return the deputies frisk the two brothers. Sean screams in pain as they pull him to his feet. "Be careful! That mother-fucker broke my arm!"

I caress Denise's back as I hold her in my arms. I mutter, "I don't remember Kansas being this fucked-up and violent."

Denise nods. "I don't think it is everywhere. I learned a lot more about Daniel's family once I was divorced. People came out of the woodwork to congratulate me on my escape. They told me tales of abuse and intimidation. More than a couple mentioned missing family members that ran foul of the Connolly family. Almost everyone else is genuinely nice - friendly and polite. The Connolly family is more like a mafia family from a bad movie."

"Isn't that just wonderful. Maybe the recorded statements from Joseph will help close some of those missing person cases," I speculate.

The sheriff walks over to Denise and me. "Topeka police are driving by her place. I'm going to call their chief." He walks away again and makes a call on his cell phone.

We wait as the sheriff talks on the phone. The deputies drag our assailants to the cars and start to question them. The sheriff joins the questioning.

Eventually, I call out. "Sheriff. Is it okay for us to go inside? We drove down from KC, and a toilet is sounding pretty good about now."

He nods, so I try to get our bags out. With the back quarter-panel caved in, the hatch of the SUV won't open.

I reach over the back seat and pull our bags over the seatback. Denise carries the toy bag and her attaché, and I carry our two suitcases. I unlock the door and Denise runs to the bathroom. I set the bags inside and hurry to the guest bathroom. After I wash up I meet Denise in the kitchen. She kisses me and hands me a glass of water. I drain that, and she takes a long pull on her glass before putting on a pot of coffee.

I pull out some coffee mugs and a carafe. We take a tray of coffee mugs and fixings out to the sheriff and his men. The sheriff is talking on his phone as we approach.

"Coffee, gentlemen?" Denise asks. Two of the officers pull big mugs out of their cars and approach with smiles on their faces. Denise says, "Looks like I better put on another pot."

I kiss her cheek and tell her, "I'll get it, Sweetheart." I set the tray on the hood of her SUV before running off to brew a second pot. I shut off the recorder on my phone, and save the file to DropBox again. I pour the coffee into my thermos and take it outside in time to hear Sheriff Eskola brief Denise. I notice our assailants and two cars are gone.

He says, "The Topeka police found your friend in her condo. The front door had been broken. They said it looked like a sledgehammer had been used. Miss Sadduzai was found unconscious in a hallway, and she appears to have been severely beaten. She's on her way to Stormont-Vail's emergency room by ambulance. Do you know any of her family?"

Denise nods, "Her father is a neurologist with Cotton-O'Neil in north Topeka, um...Muhaimin Sadduzai. Her sister is Durnaz, but I don't remember her surname. She's married, and she's an orthopedist in Topeka. Her brothers are Zahur and Ruwaihim - a pediatrician and a teacher respectively. I think I have her mom's cell phone if I can have my phone back. Her name is Liyana"

The sheriff beckons for her to follow as he returns to his truck while he finishes relaying the information Denise gave him. I pour coffee for the remaining deputy and myself while I wait. I see Denise pulling up screens on her phone. She turns it around and offers it to the sheriff. He smiles curtly and speaks into his own phone. He speaks to Denise, and she returns to cuddle up against me.

Denise sobs, "She's hurt badly, Marc. I told her your name, and that I had moved in with you. She said she wouldn't tell anyone, but..."

"Shhhhh. Denise, when someone starts beating on you, it's hard not to talk. I suspect these two were far from gentle," I explain.

Tears stream down Denise's face. "She's so sweet. Why would they do that, Marc?"

I think back to their behavior during our short time together. "They're bullies, and they feel entitled, Darling. Apparently, they've learned that they can do whatever they want with impunity."

"I want to call the prosecutors, but I don't think it would do any good. Both cases should be very straightforward," she says.

The sheriff walks over with a coffee mug. I offer to top him off while he speaks. He nods and says, "Okay, Ms. Schneider. The Topeka police reached Miss Sadduzai's mother. An ambulance took your friend to Stormont-Vail. One of my men is taking Sean Connolly to St. Francis hospital to get his arm set. Normally, they'd go to Stormont since it's closer, but I had him change given your friend is there. Topeka police will meet my deputy there and question Sean once they get him in a cast."

The sheriff takes a sip of coffee and nods. "That's about it. I've got a wrecker coming out to take their truck to our lot in Lyndon. The

KBI is getting involved due to the alleged involvement of law enforcement."

"Alleged my ass, Sheriff," I growl. "There is nothing alleged about the way they attacked us or Denise's friend."

The sheriff smirks. "I have to say 'alleged' until they're prosecuted. There is not much doubt they did the crimes."

A big tow truck pulls into the driveway. The sheriff says, "Thanks for your cooperation, folks." He ambles off to talk to the wrecker driver.

❧ 2 ❧

BREAKOUT

Sean rides to the hospital in the back of Deputy Morgan's patrol car. He's still cuffed, and he's fuming from the indignity of it.

Deputy Morgan calls in, "Taking prisoner, Sean Connolly, to St. Francis Hospital in Topeka to have his broken arm set."

The dispatcher says, "Protocol is to go to Stormont-Vail, Morgan."

"The sheriff said to take him to St. Francis due to unusual circumstances," Deputy Morgan responds.

The sheriff comes on the radio. "Dispatch, this is Sheriff Eskola. Deputy Morgan is following my orders. Please log the deviation from protocol, and send me an email reminder to document the justification."

"Roger, Sheriff," the dispatcher responds.

The rest of the drive is quiet. Sean stews and squirms, trying to make his broken arm more comfortable. He can't believe all the stupid shit that his brother Joseph revealed while lying on the ground. He thinks, *'And who the fuck is this Hough guy? The guy just danced between us like it was prom! I'll need to have the Chief check him out. Despite Joseph being a dumbass, he's right. This can't go unanswered. Hough needs to pay for this!'* A grim smile appears on Sean's face.

Deputy Morgan sees the smirk in the mirror. He wonders, *'What kind of trouble is this asshole gonna stir up next?'*

About fifteen minutes later Morgan finds a parking space close to the emergency entrance of KU Med Center, which many of the locals still call 'St. Francis Hospital.' It's only about three blocks from Stormont-Vail hospital. Morgan recalls his grandmother, a former nurse at Stormont, saying that many of the nurses at St. Francis used to be sisters in a religious order.

A Topeka patrol car parks next to him. Deputy Morgan gets out and greets the other two officers before pulling Sean out of the back seat. Morgan keeps a hand on the back of Sean's head to keep the crooked cop from banging his head on the doorframe. Once Sean is standing, Morgan follows the cute female cop, Officer Gentilly, into the ER while her partner, Officer Davis, guides Sean by his broken arm.

Officer Davis whispers to Sean, "Your brother finally got what was coming to him. He had a gorgeous, smart wife, and he beat her and ran around fucking every ugly big-titted woman he could find. If I ever find out who killed him, I'm going to thank the guy for cleaning up the gene-pool. Do something stupid today, so I can help, okay?"

Sean growls, "Brave words when I'm in cuffs."

"Says the man who beat a defenseless woman nearly to death," the cop responds. "I'm not brave, Connolly, but I do my duty and I'm a very good shot. Try me, you evil fucker."

"That's enough, Officer Davis," Deputy Morgan murmurs quietly.

Officer Davis nods as they step up to reception. Deputy Morgan says, "Hello. I'm Deputy Morgan from the Osage County Sheriff's office. I have a prisoner with a broken arm."

The receptionist nods, "Right, Deputy. We got a call about fifteen minutes ago. I understand your prisoner has insurance."

Morgan hands over Sean's insurance card while the woman notes everything on her computer. She looks up and says, "It's a slow day. We should have you in a room in a few minutes. Unfortunately, the doctors do have a severe case, so it might be a couple of hours before they get him patched up."

"No problem," Deputy Morgan says. He pulls Sean over to a seat and sits a seat away from him. The two police officers sit nearby.

Relatively quickly, a nurse guides them into a treatment room. Deputy Morgan handcuffs Sean's left arm to the bed while the nurse takes his vitals.

An orderly shows up about ten minutes later to cart Sean to X-ray. Deputy Morgan handcuffs the perp to the wheelchair and follows along. When the orderly wheels Sean back to the room after X-rays, Deputy Morgan handcuffs him to the bed again.

A large doctor with an African accent shows up shortly after the X-ray. He looks at the X-rays, probes with his fingers and Sean winces. The doctor pulls a heavy metal construction over Sean's bed. There is a triangle of metal hanging from a heavy chain.

The doctor looks at Sean and says, "This is going to suck." He's holding Sean's hand as Sean shrugs. Without warning, the doctor yanks and twists Sean's arm.

Sean screams, and the doctor nonchalantly starts poking at the broken ends and shakes his head. He looks Sean in the eye and pulls again as he pushes on one of the broken ends of the bone. He nods with satisfaction and tells Sean, "Hold onto the handle. If you move, I may have to set it again."

The doctor nods to the Deputy. "I will have a cast technician here shortly." The doctor gets up to leave, and Deputy Morgan follows him out.

"Hey, Doctor?" Morgan asks. The doctor turns around inquiringly. Morgan asks, "Is that how you normally set that type of fracture?"

The doctor grimaces. "No," he replies. "It is not. However, the Sadduzai family are friends of mine. I heard what he did to Aliyah. I chose to use a field expedient method rather than trying to be more gentle and drug him. I did not harm him, but I also didn't make it as easy on him as I could have. Sadly, my oath means I cannot punish him more severely. I'll have to leave his judgment in Allah's hands and the hands of the courts."

"Thanks, Doctor. I'll make sure he gets to court," Deputy Morgan says with a decisive nod of his head.

The cast tech arrives about thirty minutes later and builds a cast on Sean Connolly's arm from wrist to armpit. About forty-five minutes later, the bandages have set long enough for the tech to leave. The doctor arrives about twenty minutes after the tech's departure and declares Sean is ready to leave.

A nurse arrives and Deputy Morgan signs the paperwork for Sean's release from the hospital. Sean asks to use the toilet before going. The deputy escorts him to a restroom. There are no exterior windows, so he allows Sean to do his business on his own.

As the door closes, Sean looks at the ceramic lid to the toilet tank and grins. He does his business and flushes. Then he carefully lifts the heavy ceramic lid and holds it primarily in his left hand. He calls, "Coming out."

Deputy Morgan pushes the door into the room, sticking his head in. Morgan says, "Okay, let's go..." as Sean swings the heavy ceramic backhand into the unaware deputy's head. The ceramic cover breaks in half as Morgan falls to the ground.

Sean pulls the 'Deputy' windbreaker off Deputy Morgan and slides it over his cast. He snaps the jacket closed. He grabs Morgan's hat and pulls the deputy further into the bathroom. He can't shoot with his left hand, but he takes Morgan's gun regardless and hurries into the hallway and heads toward the exit.

Sean hears, "Hey! Morgan!" Sean holds a finger in the air and passes outside. He turns left as he steps outside and runs.

Officer Davis stands in the corridor. Officer Gentilly says, "Uh...Davis. Isn't that Deputy Morgan?" She scurries to the restroom that has a boot in the doorway. "Shit," she curses. "Prisoner escaped!"

"Shit!" Officer Davis exclaims as he picks up the hand mic off his shoulder. "This is Two-Charlie-Eight-Alpha. Officer down at St. Francis Emergency Room. Prisoner Sean Connolly is impersonating a sheriff's deputy in a black 'Deputy' windbreaker and grey uniform hat. Alert the detail at Stormont-Vail guarding his victim. He may be armed. I'm in pursuit on foot." He tosses the car keys to Officer Gentilly. "Follow when you can. Meet me at Stormont."

Deputy Morgan groans as he tries to sit up. "Hat."

Officer Gentilly tells him, "We saw him leave. Davis is in pursuit."

Morgan moans, "Go. I'll survive. That fucker is evil. He's going to hurt or kill someone. Stop him."

Gentilly caresses the deputy's face and winks at him just before her expression turns fierce. She runs to the front desk and grabs the nurse on duty. "Our prisoner escaped by injuring the Deputy escorting him. The Deputy is in the restroom, and he's conscious. Please help him. Notify your security that the prisoner escaped and we saw him leave. That doesn't mean he might not come back and try to hijack a ride. I gotta run."

The nurse nods sharply. "We've got this. Go!" The nurse calls out to an orderly. "Christopher, get a gurney and come with me!" She hurries down the hall to the restroom.

Officer Gentilly pulls her weapon and clears the parking lot before unlocking her unit and getting in. She locks the door and starts the car before picking up the radio. "This is Two-Charlie-Eight-Bravo. Deputy Morgan, Osage County Sheriff's Office, is conscious. ER staff are helping him. I'm in pursuit of the prisoner in our unit."

The dispatcher says, "Roger, Two-Charlie-Eight-Bravo. The detail at Stormont and hospital security have been alerted."

Gentilly hears, "Two-Charlie-Eight-Bravo, this is Two-Charlie-Eight-Alpha. The prisoner was seen running east on 7th Avenue. Take 9th across to Lane and drive north. I still haven't seen the prisoner."

"Roger, Two-Charlie-Eight-Alpha. I just passed 8th southbound. No sirens," Officer Gentilly broadcasts. She drops the microphone and turns left on 9th Avenue. She scans both sides of the street looking for Sean Connolly. She looks left, then right, then back to the left as she drives north on Lane. She doesn't see any sign of Sean Connolly, but her partner appears trotting towards her as he scans left and right.

Officer Gentilly turns left on 8th Avenue and stops.

Officer Davis jumps in and says, "Head to Stormont."

They drive west to Washburn and cross the street to park near Stormont-Vail Hospital's emergency room. Officer Gentilly asks, "What next?"

Officer Davis frowns as he stops with his hand on the handle. "The detail is up at the ICU. Let's head in and set up a room in the ER. Maybe we can get him to think we are the security detail."

She nods, and the two officers exit their car.

๛

SEAN CONOLLY RAN OUT OF THE ST. FRANCIS EMERGENCY ROOM into the parking lot. He turned left and ran to the edge of the building and then north to find another entrance to the building. He heard a voice yelling, "Connolly!"

Sean ducked down into a juniper bush near the building. He watched Davis run up to the Hispanic lady heading to the building. Davis asked, "Did you see a man in a black jacket?"

The lady pointed down to the east hesitantly, and the policeman ran off down the street. As the lady approached the building, Sean heard her ask her daughter, "*¿Qué ha dicho?*" (What did he say?)

The daughter says, "*Preguntó si habíamos visto a un hombre con una chaqueta negrón.*" (He asked about a man in a black jacket.) The mother shrugs, and they head into the hospital.

When the policeman progressed to about halfway down the block, Sean started working his way south toward the other hospital. He thought to himself, '*That Arabic reporter must be at Stormont-Vail. It's a shame her wounds are fatal. She won't be able to identify her assailants.*' He grinned as he saw the female officer whip the police car out of the parking lot heading south.

Sean jogged over to Horne street and continued toward the other hospital. He saw a large man in scrubs smoking in the parking lot. Sean angled over and addressed the large orderly. "Excuse me, sir. I'm Deputy Morgan. I need your help."

The orderly took a drag and answered as he exhaled. "Sure, Deputy. What can I..." Sean punched with the knuckles of his left hand into the guy's throat. The big orderly dropped to the ground, and Sean kicked him in the head three times.

Sean lifted the badge lanyard off the guy before he tried desperately to get the top of the scrubs off the heavy orderly. He muttered, "God-damn, I need some pain meds."

With his right arm in a cast to his armpit and his elbow immobilized at a right angle, the job was even harder than it should have been. Sean eventually managed it, and then stripped off the guy's pants, leaving him lying on the pavement in a t-shirt and a thong.

Sean noticed a puddle growing under the guy and smirked. "See, smoking will kill you, mother-fucker." He checks, and finds there is only a drop or two on the scrubs. He chuckles, "I dribble more than that when I pee."

Sean stripped off the black jacket, hat, and the flannel shirt he was wearing over the brown waffle shirt. He carefully threaded the scrubs shirt over his cast before he slipped his other arm and head into the shirt. The scrubs pants were loose enough that Sean could pull them on over his boots and cargo pants. It was just difficult with only one useful arm.

Sean lifted the badge lanyard over his head before kicking the orderly in the head again.

As Sean walked casually to the ER entrance, he heard a rattling with each step. He stopped and patted the big pockets off his hospital uniform. He twisted to get his left hand into his right pocket, and he was just able to get his hands around a small bottle. He read the label. "Vicodin," Sean muttered. "That's a real pain killer!"

Sean struggled to open the bottle, but he finally kneeled on his left knee, held the bottle in his right hand against the right knee, and opened it after four attempts. The label said one or two tablets every four to six hours. He popped three in his mouth and swallowed before closing the bottle and sliding it into his left pocket.

Sean continued making his way casually to the ER. He entered the ambulance entrance. The receptionist stopped him and said, "Take Mr. Dunlap to room nine. Here's the chart. Don't forget to give the chart to the nurse."

Sean said, "Sure." He saw a nurse place her badge on a card reader and go back into the ward. Sean called out to the reception area, "Mr. Thomas Dunlap." An old guy in a wheelchair raised his hand, and there was an equally decrepit woman with a walker standing next to him. Sean told the old woman, "Have a seat, dear. The doctor will be out to see you after he checks Mr. Dunlap. He'll be in room nine."

The old man looked up at him. "She needs to come with me."

"We don't have any place for her to sit right now," Sean murmured to him. "The doctor or nurse will get her." Sean carefully drove the wheelchair up to the door using his left hand and tried to desperately hold the record in his right. He finally got to the door, used the badge he stole to unlock the door, and pushed the old guy through. He saw an empty room, pushed the wheelchair into it and pulled the curtain.

Sean saw a gurney in the corridor with a large moaning woman sporting an oxygen tube running into her nose. There was a bag with a colorful dress in it under the gurney next to the oxygen bottle. Sean grabbed the bag and walked up to the nurses' station. He asks the charge nurse, "There was an Arabic woman. What room is she in? Her bag fell off in the room."

The nurse said, "Room 418, I think. ICU. Just look for the cops." Sean shrugged and took off toward the elevator.

Officer Davis says, "There he goes. He's in scrubs." He moves to follow Sean Connolly.

Officer Gentilly says as she follows Officer Davis, "I'll call it in." She picks up her microphone and says, "Prisoner spotted in the Stormont ER walking to the north tower elevators. He's wearing blue scrubs with a brown waffle shirt underneath. He has a visible cast holding his right arm at a right angle.

Officer Davis stops and calls out, "Connolly! Stop!" He dashes towards the elevator as Sean steps inside.

Sean pushes the 'close' button and holds it until the elevators start moving upward. He mutters, "Fuckers. You bitches don't stand a chance against a Connolly. This raghead bitch is already dead."

3

DENISE'S FRIEND

The sheriff called a wrecker for our attackers' pickup, but we had to call another wrecker to haul off Denise's SUV. We empty the glovebox and console of Denise's belongings and wait for it to arrive. Denise rents a car through her insurance app while we wait.

The wrecker loads her Infiniti onto the bed and takes it off to the Nissan dealership in Topeka. We jump in my pickup and drive to the hospital.

We find the Information Desk at the front entrance and learn that Aliya is in room 418 in the intensive care unit, or ICU. We make our way to the waiting room for the ICU.

Denise gasps when we arrive and hurrys to hug an older, attractive, woman in a hijab - I'm assuming it's her friend's mother. Then she hugs a younger version standing next to the mother - maybe Aliyah's sister. Denise had told me Aliyah was Pakistani. I had no thought about her potentially being attractive, but based on the two specimens Denise is talking to, Aliyah is at least very pretty, too.

Denise introduces me to Aliyah's mother, Liyana Sadduzai, and Aliyah's sister, Durnaz Benedín

"Peace be upon you both," I tell them.

Liyana responds with a bright smile, "May the peace, mercy, and blessings of Allah be upon you, Marcus Hough." She offers a hand. "I'm glad you used English. Pakistani proper customs are very rigid and formal, and Urdu has linguistic complexities." I'm surprised to hear a posh and proper English accent.

I clasp her hand and release it as I nod, "I got into trouble in Afghanistan a few times for using the incorrect form of address based on the dialect of the person I was speaking to. I eventually figured that if they spoke English, greeting them with the proper sentiment in my language was probably acceptable. It served me pretty well. Otherwise, I was on high alert to pick up on which form my translator used. I regret we are meeting under these circumstances."

Liyana nods, "The circumstances are far from ideal. Please. Sit with us."

As I settle into a seat, I see a familiar figure in scrubs and a cast casually walking toward the door the policemen were guarding.

I murmur, "Excuse me," as I launch out of my chair. I hurry to follow, and I see Sean Connolly approaching the guard detail. I call out, "Connolly! Freeze!" He stutter-steps and continues toward the guard. I run towards my former attacker.

The slender black police officer on the near side of the door holds out a hand to stop Connolly. The officer does put a hand on his pistol, but doesn't draw it. The larger white cop on duty with him is down at the nurse's station looking at what's happening from several feet away.

Connolly drops a pistol from his left hand as he tries to pull it from his scrubs. He improvises by grabbing the officer's hand with his left and twisting outward and down to bend the officer over. He body-checks the officer, knocking him to the ground. The other officer pulls his taser and comes running. Connolly curses and turns to run back in my direction.

I hear an authoritative voice behind me call out "Connolly" just as I close with him. I slide to the right past his broken right arm and throw a 'ridge hand' across his throat as I launch past him.

The blade of my inner forearm impacts Sean Connolly's throat, and the result is much like the vampire Selene gets in the Underworld movies.

Connolly makes a gasping, choking sound as the bone of my arm crushes his throat, and his feet fly forward as his body lifts upward slightly until he's nearly parallel to the ground. Then he drops like a rock.

I back up and stand ready as two more Topeka cops, a tall black male and a shorter blond female, run up with weapons pointing at Connolly. The female holsters her weapon and pulls her taser instead. She looks at me and says, "Sir, back off. Go sit in the waiting area until we come take a statement from you."

"Yes, ma'am," I respond and go rejoin Denise and the Sadduzai family in the waiting room.

Denise asks, "Was that Sean?"

I nod bleakly as I sit and hold her hand. "Yeah. Wearing scrubs and a cast. I wonder how he got away from the deputies and got to Topeka."

Denise says, "The sheriff said they were taking him to St. Francis to get his arm fixed because Aliyah is here."

I frown. "That's only about three blocks from here."

There is a commotion in the hallway as I hear someone yell, "Code Blue."

"What does that mean?" I ask.

"A patient isn't breathing," Durnaz says matter-of-factly as she gets up and peeks into the hallway.

She comes back and sits down. "Apparently it is an orderly. There are two policmen guarding Aliyah's room, and there are four people working on the orderly while two more policemen watch over them."

I say, "That's no orderly. That's one of the men that attacked your sister. I just crushed his throat."

Denise gets up and crawls into my lap and cradles my head against her lovely bosom. She kisses my forehead and tells me, "Don't fret it, my love. He earned that or worse. At least you weren't hurt."

A tall Asian man in a coat and tie walks into the waiting room. The Sadduzai ladies rush to him, and he collects them into a hug. Denise and I get up and join them.

I overhear him say in an English accent, "She is in a coma, and I want to keep her there for forty-eight hours. Her attending agrees. She has swelling in her cranium; although, it does not look like she currently has an active bleeder. We are hopeful that with time the swelling will reduce. We will try to wake her in a few days."

Liyana bursts into tears and hangs off the man. He looks at me while holding his wife and asks, "Who are you?"

"Peace be upon you, Doctor Sadduzai," I answer. "I am Marus Hough. This is my girlfriend Denise Schneider."

"Upon you peace, Mr. Hough," he says. "I know Denise. Why are you here?"

Denise jumps in to explain, "Muhaimin, the men that attacked Aliyah came to kill us. Marcus stopped them. After the police left our place, we came here to see how Aliyah is doing.

The tall doctor nods. "Thank you for catching them. Is that one of them lying on the floor?"

I nod, "Sadly. I don't know how he got here. He was in custody the last time I saw him."

The blond police woman walks up and says, "He hit Deputy Morgan in the head with the ceramic lid off a toilet tank and ran." She looks me in the eye. "I need to get a statement from you, sir."

She indicates a pair of chairs facing each other, so I take a seat. She sits across from me with a notepad and pen. I start the recording app on my phone. She looks at it curiously for a moment and says, "I am Officer Gentilly from the Topeka police. Tell me what happened."

Denise sits down next to me and holds my left hand in both of hers. "We had just finished up with the sheriff's men and gotten Denise's car hauled off." I point to Denise. "My girlfriend, Denise Schneider, wanted to come up here and see how her friend Aliyah, the patient in the room, is doing. During the events in Carbondale, we came to the realization that the only person we had told about us being together was Aliyah Sadduzai. It wasn't much of a leap to figure out the Connolly brothers went to beat on her to gain information about us."

The officer raises her hand, and I stop. She says, "Jump forward to when you arrived at the hospital."

I scratch my head for a moment. "Well, we arrived and parked out front. We stopped at the Information Desk to find out what room

Aliyah was in and came up here. Denise introduced me to Mrs. Sadduzai and Mrs. Benedín. We were about to sit down and share what we know when I saw Sean Connolly walking by in a cast, light blue scrubs, and a brown waffle shirt under the scrubs top. I noticed he had the same boots on as before, which was the final confirmation I had the right guy."

I pause a moment to ensure I have events in the correct order. "I saw Connolly approaching the police officer on guard duty, so I called out for him to stop. I think I said, 'Connolly. Freeze.' He paused for just an instant, and the officer on duty stuck out a hand to stop him. Connolly tried to pull a pistol out of his scrubs, but he dropped it. Then he did something to the officer that caused the officer to fall. The other officer on guard duty pulled a taser and charged toward Connolly. Connolly turned back to me, and I heard someone, I think it was your partner, call out for Connolly to stop. He didn't. I launched off his line of escape and threw my arm across his throat with the intent of stopping him. Once he hit the floor I backed off, and you told me to take a seat." I nod to myself as I finish my summary.

The policewoman looks at me curiously for a moment and puts her notebook away. She points at my phone and waves her fingers across her throat. I shrug and stop the recording. I save it to DropBox and set the phone aside.

Officer Gentilly asks quietly, "Are you the guy that killed Daniel Connolly?"

I answer, "He died of injuries sustained when I tried to prevent him from hurting Ms. Schneider and myself."

The young police woman grabs my right hand in both of hers and gives it a firm squeeze.

"Thank you," she says. "He had sexual relationships with a couple of handfuls of women either on the force or in administration, but he accosted a lot more. He always did it in such a way that it would have been a 'he said / she said' situation. For all of us that were in fear of him, you have our deepest gratitude."

Denise says, "Daniel was a piece of shit. I couldn't believe the things I learned about him and his family after our divorce. As bad as he was, his brothers are worse. Their father is the Chief of Police in

Salina, and I understand he condones their behavior. Meeting Marcus just underlined how bad of a husband Daniel was."

Denise takes a breath before telling Officer Gentilly, "Aliyah asked me to meet her at the library Friday afternoon. We sat in a conference room, and she interviewed me about what happened with Daniel on Tuesday, what led up to it, and what the aftermath has been like. I told her Marcus' name and that we are living together outside of Carbondale. I had managed to get a court order to seal the record of Tuesday's incident due to the danger Marcus would be in if the Connolly family ever found him. Thankfully, I told Aliyah enough to get them to leave her alive."

"How is the Deputy that took Connolly to the hospital?" I ask.

Officer Gentilly eyes moisten as she says, "I don't know. I need to check on him. I turned him over to the nurse at KU hospital and chased after Connolly." I look at her puzzled, so she clarifies. "St. Francis hospital."

I ask her, "Would you please contact Sheriff Eskola in Osage County and let him know that his Deputy was injured in the line of duty."

Officer Gentilly releases my hand. "Let me go do that. Thanks for your time."

It sounds like there is still a lot of commotion in the hallway, so we sit still.

I tell the Sadduzai family, "As soon as I get confirmation that the police don't need anything else, we need to go. We need to get Denise a rental car, and we both need to get ready for work tomorrow."

Aliyah's father shakes my hand. "Thank you for doing all you could for my daughter, Mr. Hough."

"Please, call me Marcus," I tell him.

"I am 'Muhaimin,' and you may call my wife 'Liyana,' if you wish," Dr. Sadduzai says.

"It's my honor, Muhaimin, Liyana. Please keep us informed of Aliyah's condition," I say.

I check with Officer Gentillly, and she says we can leave. I see Connolly on a gurney, and several medical professionals are taping a tracheostomy tube into his throat, checking his vitals, *etcetera*.

Denise and I wave to the Sadduzai family and walk back to my truck.

We stop at the car rental agency on the way home, and Denise picks up a small Buick SUV to drive on her commute while we get the insurance and repairs for her Infinity addressed. I follow Denise home.

Upon our return, we immediately tumble into bed for some life-affirming sex.

Denise opens my pants and slides my hard cock in her mouth. She voraciously devours my cock for a couple of minutes - sucking and licking the top quarter before graduating to bobbing up and down. I whip off my shirt as she drives her lips to my torso and my cock slides into the constricting depths of her throat. Denise pops up off me, and she removes her sweater and bra. She captures my cock between her generous breasts and presses them together around my flesh. She slides my cock in-and-out the warm silky tunnel of her décolletage, sucking my cock into her mouth as it emerges from her breasts.

Denise doesn't keep that up for long. She says, "That's hard on my back."

"Feels wonderful, Pet. Next time you lay down and let me move," I tell her.

"Yes, Sir. That sounds wonderful," she moans.

She shimmies out of her yoga pants as I kick out of my own pants. I follow Denise as she crawls backwards on the bed. I roll her up on her side and push the top leg towards her chest, allowing me to slide into the sexy wet folds of her pussy.

We made love passionately for long enough that I had two orgasms. I lost track of how many Denise had.

Afterward we shower together. Once we're clean, I call Dad while Denise and I whip up soup, sauteed spinach, and sandwiches for a late dinner. I put Dad on speaker, and he immediately asks if we are okay. Denise and I explain that we thought we might come see him this evening, but that we didn't due to the attack. He tells us tomorrow is soon enough. He seems like he's having a good day. He asks a lot of questions about what happened but they all seem on point, and he doesn't repeat any. I promise to come see him tomorrow.

Dad finally says, "Here you go."

There are some scuffling sounds, then I hear a clear female voice. "Hello?"

I respond with as much intelligence as I possibly can. "Uh...hello. This is Marcus Hough."

"Oh!" the voice exclaims. "Hello, Mr. Hough. Gretchen Osborn here. Your father just handed me the phone." She giggles cutely.

I chuckle, "I'm not sure why, Gretchen."

She says brightly, "I think he's just tired. Kevin and I just walked in to check on him. Kevin's going to get him ready for bed." She turns away from the phone, and I hear her say, "Carl, Marcus says 'goodnight.'" Then I hear Dad say loudly, "Goodnight, son!"

"Goodnight, Carl," Gretchen says away from the phone. Then she resumes talking to me. "That was it, Mr. Hough. I'm taking the phone back to the front desk."

"Okay, Gretchen. Have a good night," I tell her.

"You too, sir," she says. Then there is a beep, and I hear her gasp. "God! He's so sweet!"

I chuckle and hang up.

Denise smirks at me. "Seems like you have a fan, Marc."

I chuckle, "Yes, all the inappropriately young ladies think I'm hot."

Denise laughs. "Gretchen is legal. The weekend I met your dad, I heard her talking to another aide at the nursing home about how dreamy you are - her words. She got rather embarrassed when she realized I was your girlfriend."

I shake my head, "She'll grow out of it as soon as some football player or young graduate student makes googly eyes at her. She's got that whole young wholesome athletic thing going. It won't be long."

"Maybe," Denise says. "Something tells me she's going to be slow to let her dreams go. She is really cute, though. I can't imagine she doesn't have a fan club at the university."

"I'm your fan club, Denise."

"Yes, you are," she agrees.

⚘ 4 ⚘

RESEARCH

Monday, Denise went to work after we shared breakfast. She left me with a kiss.

I visited Dad shortly after his breakfast. He was a little befuddled but overall not too bad.

After I bid Dad *bon appetit* for his lunch, I called a local prepper from the parking lot. I asked if he would be okay if I dropped by after lunchtime to discuss home protection. He agreed.

The only reason I know Roy Fields is that I went to school with his son Gerry. His daughter, Shelly, was a year ahead of me in school. I wasn't close with either of them, but my dad had visited Roy several times to discuss farming. Dad mentioned a couple of times that Roy had an extensive weapon collection and was a 'gun nut.' I translated that into 'survivalist' or 'prepper' over the years, but I've never done more than exchange pleasantries with him at the store since I moved back.

I grabbed a quick lunch at Four Corners restaurant and then drove over to Roy's house. I ended up talking to Roy for about two hours as he went on a rant about gun laws, communists, liberals, and the government in general. He also took me to his range with a wheelbarrow full of weapons. He had dug a decent 200-yard range into an old strip mine on his property. I fired nine-mil, ten-mil, five-seven, and forty-five caliber automatic pistols, plus a .357 magnum revolver. Then I fired a 20-gauge and a 12-gauge shotgun, a 12-gauge bull-pup, and a weapon I hadn't seen before that looks like an AR-15 rifle but is actually classified as a pistol.

I didn't have a preference for any of the weapons. I've alway just considered weapons to be tools. I got the impression that there is a fair amount of sexual gratification for Roy from his guns. I did pull a couple of nuggets out of our conversation. I decided I probably want at least one semi-automatic shotgun and a pistol each for Denise and I. We'll need to get 'concealed carry' certified, too. It's not required unless we want to travel, but the Plaza in Kansas City is in Missouri. Denise and I both want to go back there. I wonder what Denise will think about all this. I'll also need to get gun safes installed in each car and the house. Roy refers me to the Gun Garage in north Topeka and Charger Arms in Osage City. The former has an indoor range and classes.

I thanked Roy for his time and headed home to let his advice percolate while I worked out on tire exercises and karate forms in the machine shed.

After a quick rinse in the shower, I continued work on the Buffalo Soldiers book for a couple of hours. The content was riveting, but the writing style was distracting. I also found a couple of things that sounded like quotes, but they weren't sourced. I marked up the document heavily for writing style. By the time I called it 'quits,' another twelve-to-sixteen hours of work remained to finish the job.

If the writer isn't offended by me trying to clean up his style, I'll probably get a request for a second edit after re-writes. It's the first time I've worked with this guy, so I'm not really certain what to expect.

I WRAP UP WORK AND GIVE DAD A QUICK CALL BEFORE GETTING MY bag ready for karate class. I text Denise to remind her about class, and I get a call back immediately.

"Hi, Marc. Can you stay home tonight?" she asks. *"I'm a little freaked out by all the crap the Connollys have been pulling."*

"Okay, Love. I'll put some dinner on," I agree.

"I'll text you when I leave," she says. *"I love you, Marc."*

"I love you too, Denise," I answer. I hear her disconnect.

I jump in my truck and head into Carbondale to grab some groceries. The small local store isn't anything like the big supermarkets in Flagstaff, Phoenix, or even Topeka, but they have plenty of the basics and some surprising variety. I get a beef roast, a couple of steaks, some pasta, and a bunch of different vegetables. After packing my groceries in the truck, I detour to one of the liquor stores to pick up some wine - the damned ancient blue laws in Kansas don't allow the grocer to carry anything decent. I find a decent Shiraz and a questionable Pinot Noir. They do have a couple of New Zealand Sauvignon Blancs that seem decent, so I grab all of that, a twelve-pack of Stella Artois, and a pint of 'Old No. 7' Jack Daniels.

I carry that to the truck and haul my treasures home. I get a text from Denise as I'm carrying the groceries in from the garage. I send her an acknowledgement before I put everything away. I fry some onions and potatoes, sautée some mushrooms and onions with a splash of the Shiraz, sautée some frozen spinach with onions, and season the steaks. I'm a big fan of onions and skillets. I drop two crushed cloves of garlic into about two tablespoons of olive oil to pour over the spinach. I put the mushroom mix into a pyrex bowl and set it in the oven at 125 degrees to keep it warm. I toss the garlic oil in the spinach and give it the same treatment as the mushrooms.

I check the door and decide I have about ten-to-fifteen minutes before Denise gets home. I put a cast iron skillet on a medium fire to heat while I set the table. I pour a couple glasses of the Shiraz, and I hear her pull in the garage as I set down the bottle.

I pull on my boots and walk out. I collect a kiss from my lady, and Denise moans into my mouth as I give her firm ass a squeeze. I release the hot, ripe woman in my arms and walk around to the passenger seat to grab her attaché case. I notice she didn't do yoga today. I also notice an open pistol case on the seat with an automatic pistol resting there.

Denise looks at me through the driver's side window, biting her lip.

I smirk as I say, "Well, that conversation is going to go easier than I anticipated. What is it?"

She shakes her head. "Walther PPQ nine-mil. You want to talk to me about carrying?"

"Yep, but after dinner," I tell her. "The skillet ought to be hot enough for me to throw the steaks on. I'll let you clear your own weapon, Love."

"Pink, no blood," she says as she reaches inside the vehicle. I stop in the doorway and cock an eyebrow at her, and she laughs. "My steak, goofball."

I smirk and carry her satchel inside. I set it where she staged it last night before putting the steaks on.

During dinner, Denise says, "With all the violence in the last week, I thought I should start carrying again. Shooting was one of the few things Daniel and I did together. I have a concealed carry permit, and I used to train regularly. I've only been to the range twice since the divorce."

"Why didn't you pull it when Daniel attacked last Tuesday?" I ask gently.

"I don't know," she says. "I already had it packed in my suitcase at the time. My purse was right there on the coffee table, so I went to the pepper spray instead. I didn't think about the gun until Daniel started shooting. It was over so quickly after that point that getting the gun would have been pointless."

I nod before I tell her about my experience. "According to the counselors I talked to, there are two common responses to firearms after being in combat. One is to stock up on guns because you'll never feel safe without a weapon. The other is to avoid them. There are a lot of folks that fall somewhere in between, but those are the boundaries. I had learned to defend myself without guns before I joined the military, and I steered away from them after I got out. I also learned how to shoot as a kid - pretty typical growing up on a farm. Dad sold his .30-06 but left his semi-automatic .22 rifle here when he went into the nursing home, so I have that. I need to clean it, but it's not really a great home defense weapon. It can work, but not ideal." I take a bite of steak.

"What are you thinking about getting?" Denise asks before she pushes her hair behind her ear and cuts off a bite of steak.

I shrug as I finish chewing. "I'm thinking we both should start carrying pistols. I want to get at least one shotgun, too. Maybe an AR-15 or AR-10 rifle."

Denise nods as she chases her steak with a sip of wine. Eventually she says, "My mom and dad both used to be in a 'hunt club' in Salina. I grew up shooting shotguns at clay pigeons - both trap and skeet. I can shoot up to a 12-gauge pretty well. I don't like the 10-gauge - too much recoil."

"I've really only used rifles and pistols regularly despite being trained on many different weapons in the army," I admit. "I've got a lot to learn."

Denise says, "The range I used to go to is off Meridien in north Topeka."

"Yeah, I was looking at that one online. Do you want to go up there tomorrow after you finish work?" I ask.

"Sounds good," Denise agrees. "Let's finish this wonderful meal, so I can properly thank Sir for spoiling me."

I grin, "Part of the full service I provide, Pet."

Denise giggles, and after a few bites she asks, "What did you do today?"

"I visited Dad in the morning, had lunch at Four Corners, and met with a local gun enthusiast to get his opinions on home defense," I tell her. She looks interested, so I continue. "In between informing me of all his conspiracy theories, he let me fire a variety of weapons. He had some interesting ones, but I can't say why I might pick one over another."

Denise nods, "We can go relatively inexpensive until you find what you like. I figured the military-style rifles would appeal to you more than standard hunting weapons."

I nod, "Yeah. I routinely qualified 'Expert' in M-16 and M9 in the service. I've used both to ki...I've used both effectively in combat." I pause a moment to think back on that, but quickly decide it's an exercise of diminishing returns. "Regardless, I played with Roy for a couple of hours, came back and worked out in the shed for a bit, showered, and worked on the Buffalo Soldiers book for a couple of hours. I'll have it done this week." I raise my wineglass in her direction. "How about your day?"

She nods. "I called Liyana today for an update on Aliyah. So far their taking a 'no news is good news' approach. She said Muhaimin said today's imaging showed no increase in swelling and maybe a little diminishing. They're hopeful that tomorrow will show some significantly reduced swelling. Then they'll try to bring her out of the coma. I told her I'd call back tomorrow." She pushes her plate away and sips her wine. "Other than that, I turned that opinion from last week over to the Chief Justice, and I'm pulling some research for her on two other cases. One is a really demented twist trying to get around Roe v. Wade - essentially removing a woman's sovereignty over her body on religious grounds. This one may get kicked up to Federal."

"Honestly, I think the only way to stop these misogynist attacks is to put laws into effect that require men to be licensed to have sex. That's the only way some guys will ever get it," I say.

That gets a chuckle from Denise.

After dinner, I clean up the kitchen, and Denise pulls a folder out of her satchel to catch up on a couple of things she needs to be on top of tomorrow.

I refill her wine glass and ask, "How long, Pet?"

She looks up at me as I set the bottle down and slide a hand inside her blouse to fondle her breasts. She moans, "Much longer if Sir keeps doing that. Thirty minutes otherwise, Sir."

I pinch her nipple and lean down for a kiss. I release her lips, "If I have to come find you, I'll have to treat you like a naughty girl, Denise."

I pull her nipple insistently, and Denise moans at the stimulation. "Oh, Sir! I am your naughty girl."

I bite her ear gently before letting her get back to work. "Hurry, Pet. I've missed you," I whisper to her.

She smiles brightly as she turns her eyes back to her work. I see headlights turn into the driveway.

I murmur, "Company."

Denise retrieves her weapon. She clears it, function checks it, and loads it. She jacks a round into the chamber. She murmurs, "I'm live, Marc."

The security lights off the machinery shed are on, and I see the Sheriff's pickup pull to a stop by the back patio. I grab a boning knife and walk to the door. I turn on the porch lights, and Denise takes up position across the living room from the door with the weapon pointed out the window towards the door. I put the knife in my left hand and prepare to open the door.

Sheriff Eskola walks up to the door, and I open it before he knocks. He's suddenly wary. I greet him. "Hello, Sheriff. How may we help you this evening?"

He looks pointedly at the knife and says, "You could start by putting that knife away."

I tell him, "We've been attacked twice in a week. I think a little caution is called for."

The sheriff nods, "Understandable. Especially since I came in after dark. I locked my sidearm in the safe in my truck." He raises his hand. He has a collapsible baton, but no firearm or taser.

"Come on in, Sheriff," I tell him. I back out of the way and set the knife on a side table.

I say, "Clear, Denise." The sheriff steps in and takes notice of Denise lifting the muzzle of her weapon to point away from him before setting it next to her favorite chair on the magazine table.

The sheriff mutters, "Damn! You two really are jumpy."

"Yes, Sheriff," Denise admits. "I had to hide from an abusive ex-husband in my last house, and I thought I would be safe out here in the country with Marcus. Two of the biggest boogie-men from my past attacked us here. I'm not a very happy woman."

"We'll make you happy in a little bit, Pet." My comment takes her out of time for a moment, and then she flashes me a big smile.

She murmurs with big doe eyes, "I can't wait, Sir."

"Uh...," the sheriff begins as he watches the interplay between Denise and myself. "Um, I came by to drop off your mail. The Connolly boys took it from your mailbox, but we didn't find it until we processed the truck this morning. I got permission to bring it by once we documented the evidence with the Lyndon postmaster and the

FBI. That means that in addition the assault charges and attempted vehicular homicide charges from us, and the attempted murder and assaulting a police officer in Topeka, they've now got federal mail-tampering charges."

Denise chuckles, "That's the one that's likely going to hurt them the most."

The sheriffs smiles tentatively. "I don't know. Either way, I've been entertaining KBI and FBI all day today." He hands me the mail and takes off his hat. He scratches his scalp for a moment. "Mr. Hough, Ms. Schneider, I understand there are two other Connolly's out there. It might be good if you can find another place to stay."

I explain, "My dad is in Brookside in Overbrook with dementia and Alzheimer's. He doesn't do well if he doesn't see me regularly. Besides, this is my childhood home. I should be safer here than anywhere else."

Sheriff Eskola says, "The security lights are good, but you have no dog. You only have one pistol in the house with how many rounds."

"One hundred," Denise says. "We also have a .22 rifle with..."

"...about three hundred..." I interject.

"...about three hundred rounds," Denise finishes.

The sheriff asks, "Do you know Roy Fields?"

I nod, "I'm acquainted with him. He let me try some of his collection today after I explained why I was interested in guns."

The sheriff shakes his head, "Don't buy anything from him. The ATF has crawled up his aaaa...shorts more than a couple of times for violations. He's sold weapons that have been associated with crimes. He picks them up somewhere cheap and sells them. In short, use a reputable dealer." The sheriff hands me a business card. "Martin Greenbaum in Scranton is a low-key dealer. He follows all the rules, but he is a prepper. He's got a focus on the types of weapons you might find useful. I personally like a clip-fed 12-gauge or a bull-pup. Martin is also a gunsmith as well as a dealer. He can build you something special to suit your needs and keep you close enough to the boundary of what's legal that you can stay out of trouble unless you go looking for it."

"Thanks, Sheriff," I tell him as I take the card. "I appreciate it."

The sheriff looks at Denise. "Do you know how to use that, ma'am?"

She grins at him, "Certified and trained, Sheriff. With a pistol I'm only good for about seventeen bulleyes out of twenty at twenty-five meters. I'm better with a shotgun."

The sheriff's squints at her. "Be careful, counsellor. I may have to enlist you as a deputy."

"Happy to serve, Sheriff. You do know my man was an MP, right?" she asks.

"Uh, no. I didn't know that," the sheriff answers as he looks at me. "Why aren't you working in law enforcement?"

I shrug, "I like writing and editing. Doesn't mean I don't train to protect me and mine."

The sheriff looks back and forth between us for a moment. Finally he says, "I don't have a reserve deputy program, but you two are welcome to join us at the range if you would like to."

I nod, "That would be great, Sheriff. Keep us posted on when that might be."

Denise asks, "How is your injured deputy, Sheriff?"

Sheriff Eskola nods grimly, "Doing okay. They let him go home this afternoon. He'll be back to work next week. Your friend's father is going to check him out Friday, but he's expected to get permission to return to duty. The doctors wrote him sick for a couple of days off to catch up on sleep. Hospitals are no place to sleep." He puts his hat on his head. "That's it for me. I need to get home to Burlingame before the wife locks me out. Have a good night."

I show the sheriff out and watch as he walks to his truck. He starts the vehicle and takes the driveway to the road. Denise clears her weapon and says conversationally, "I like dogs."

I chuckle. "Me too, Pet. I grew up with dogs and cats. Both stayed outside. Animals outside, people inside."

Denise kisses me on her way back to the kitchen table to resume her work. She murmurs into my mouth, "Works for me." She puts her pistol in its carry bag and tucks it back into her valise.

I tell her, "Thirty minutes, Pet. Clock starts now." I dramatically check my watch, and then put the boning knife away.

I figure it's early enough to call the gun dealer the sheriff recommended, so I ring him from my cell.

I hear someone answer, but no one says anything. I say, "Marcus Hough for Martin Greenbaum."

"*Speaking,*" a voice says. I immediately get the feeling this guy is paranoid.

"Sheriff Eskola referred me to you for a home protection problem. Are you available tomorrow?" I ask.

"*Are you calling from a cell phone?*"

"Yes," I answer.

"*Okay. Bye.*" He hangs up. I look at the phone trying to figure out what just happened.

I'm about to ring him back when I get a text. I check, and it's the same number that I just called. The text reads, '13:00 CDT, 38d47'54.2"N 95d45'03.5"W.' I pull up my MacBook and look up the coordinates, and I send them to my phone. I finish by sending back a text to Mr. Greenbaum, 'Roger, out.'

I wash my wine glass in the kitchen and put it in the dishwasher. I grab a couple glasses of water and take them to the bedroom. The water glasses go on the nightstands, and I pull out a couple of wooden clothespins and a paddle with leather on one side and fur on the other.

Denise asked about spanking before, so I bought the paddle. I have a riding crop, too. I suspect I'll probably use my hand on her ass if she's late. I hate to waste the opportunity to smack her perfect ass with my hand, but the paddle can have a psychological impact. Then again, she might show up on time. I strip off my clothes, set my phone alarm for the morning, brush my teeth and sit on the bed reading a book on my Kindle.

At the twenty-nine minute mark, I hear Denise running the sink. Then I hear her rattling around in the kitchen. I notice the lights dim toward the front of the house.

Denise walks into the bedroom with her pistol wearing only stockings and her heels. She puts the pistol in the nightstand and then slides on top of the comforter. She lays prone with her chin on her hands looking at me innocently, gently kicking her heels in the air.

She says in a tiny little voice, "Sir, I've been a naughty girl today."

"What happens to naughty girls, Pet?"

Denise whispers, "They get spanked, Sir." She bites her lip, knowing what that does to my cock, and then she watches to ensure her gesture gets the expected result.

I smirk before responding. She smiles brightly at me as I say, "Oh, yes they do, Pet."

5

PROTECTIVE MEASURES

I pick up the paddle and sit with my feet off the edge of the bed. "Over my knee, Pet."

Denise whimpers as she crawls across the bed to stand next to my knees.

I tell her, "Let's move, Pet. This isn't the main event. I intend to use you harshly tonight." She continues her whimpers as she bends over my knees.

I cinch her in place with my left hand as I rub the fur-covered side of the paddle across Denise's squirming ass. She whines, "Oh, Sir! I'm so excited!"

I set the paddle aside and massage her perfect ass with my hand. I squeeze each cheek, and Denise moans. When she is really feeling it, I spank her with four strokes on each cheek. I only spank her at about half strength; I only want to give her a little sting. I see tears streaming down her face, but she is not sobbing. When I stick my fingers between her thighs I find her pussy is soaked.

I suck Denise's juices off my fingers before stroking her pink ass flesh with the furry side of the paddle.

"How are you doing, Pet?"

"Oh, Sir! You spanked me so hard, but I'm so excited!" she exclaims. "It's confusing but arousing."

"Good, Denise," I tell her. "On your hands and knees in the center of the bed, my beautiful Pet."

"Yes, Sir." She gets off my lap and crawls into place.

I kneel beside the bed and pull about four feet of silk rope off a coil I recently tucked under the bed and cut it with the shears I recently added to the bottom drawer of my nightstand. I use the rope to bind Denise's hands and tie her to the headboard. She stays on her knees.

I play with her nipples until they are as hard as I've ever seen them. At that point, I apply the wooden clothespins to her turgid nipples.

"Oh, Sir!" Denise moans. She's dripping wet.

I carefully hang a two-ounce fishing weight on a lightweight three-inch chain from each clothespin. I lay down with my face between her knees and pull her dripping pussy onto my face.

I suckle her outer labia before lapping at her dripping channel. I suckle her inner petals and her juices run down my face. I stick a finger in her channel and pump it in-and-out as I start licking her clit.

Denise's whimpering intensifies, "Oh! Sir! You're driving me crazeeeeeeeee! NNNNNNNnnnnnh!"

My fingers are soaked in her swampy pussy. I give her another finger and suck her clit into my mouth. I look up her torso to see the weights swinging from her breasts and her head is looking down to catch my eyes. I wink as I suckle and lash her with my tongue, and she squeals again. "NNNNNNNNNNNNNNNNNNNNNnnnnnnnnnhh!"

I crawl out from underneath Denise and enter her from behind. She starts squirting after a couple of strokes. It's almost too much all at once. I fist my hand in her hair as I hold her with the other hand and slam into her gushing pussy. I manage to hold off my own release for a few more strokes before I come inside Denise.

After I come back to my brain, I remove the clothespins. Denise gasps as circulation returns to her nipples. Despite wanting to stay buried in her sweet pussy, I pull out and waddle around her to untie her hands.

Denise collapses to the mattress. I stretch her out flat on the bed and massage her shoulders. She rolls over at my direction and I work her shoulders some more. Finally, I roll her back over again and rub lotion into her tushy.

I pull Denise onto my chest. She throws a leg over mine, and we cuddle for a while. Eventually, she says, "I need to pee, Sir."

"Go ahead, Pet." I sit up to clear a path and wave an arm toward the bathroom. She runs off like a shot, holding her breasts to keep them from bouncing.

After I hear a flush and the running sink, she runs back to bed and crawls under the covers as I take my turn in the bathroom. When I return to bed and slide under the covers, Denise crawls onto my chest.

"What did you think, Denise."

"That was more brutal than anything we've done before," she says. I nod and she continues. "The clothespins were too tight. They felt great until they came off," she says.

I nod and say, "That is an unfortunate side effect. I can get some with lighter or adjustable springs. I'll have to order them. You may not like them as much."

She nods, "I would like to try. I did like the weights. It was freaky how they pulled my nipples as I moved. I would like to do that again."

"Good," I say in acknowledgement. "How about the spanking?"

"That was intense, too. You were holding back, weren't you?" she asked.

"Yes," I admit. "I was afraid I would hurt you if I didn't."

"I enjoyed it," Denise purrs. "I loved the entire experience, Marc."

I tell her, "I can get lost in pleasuring you in oh so many ways, Denise. I love a good kinky session with my Pet, but I revel in our vanilla time together. Making love to you as a partner, holding you, making love gently or vigorously. It doesn't matter."

I pause. "I know it sounds saccharine sweet, but...I love you, Denise Schneider."

"I love you too, Marcus Hough," she says. "I love being your pet, I love being used by you harshly, I love when you tie me up and treat me like a sex toy, and I love making plain vanilla love to you, too."

"Vanilla is actually one of my favorite flavors," I murmur with a grin.

Denise kisses me. "Mine, too. Sleep well, Sir," she murmurs sleepily.

"You too, Beloved," I assure her.

❦

THE NEXT MORNING, I DRIVE DENISE TO WORK IN THE MORNING. She has me walk her to the door, so I can keep her weapon despite my protests. I detour to 21st Street west of Gage on the way back. I remember Dad taking my brother and me to Daylight Donuts when we were little. Now there is a Dunkin one block away, but Dad always liked Daylight better. I pick up a couple of cinnamon rolls and a couple of apple fritters, which I take directly to Dad down in Overbrook at the nursing home.

I see Gretchen as I walk in. She blushes as she says, "Good morning, Mr. Hough."

"Good morning, Gretchen," I respond and give her a smile that hopefully doesn't embarrass her as I remember her comment on the phone.

I find Dad sitting at his normal breakfast table. His buddies have already gone off to watch TV, so I grab a cup of coffee and sit next to him. Dad's a little slow today, but his memory seems to be working decently. He lights up when he sees the bag from Daylight Donuts.

Dad asks about the recent attackers. I tell him there is no news other than the mail fraud charges against our attackers. Half the mail they took was Dad's, but he doesn't seem too worried about it. He is more interested in cutting his donuts in half. He has me get him a plate from the coffee station. He puts half of each of his donuts on the plate and looks around for some of the aides. Kevin and Gretchen are checking on the other residents, but Dad recognizes them as 'his people' and waves them over.

I smile and cut my donuts in half. I whisper to Dad, "Give them each a plate. You and I can share mine."

Gretchen comes to see what Dad wants. "Here's a plate for you and one for Kevin."

Gretchen flashes him a winning smile. "Why thank you, Carl.

That's very sweet." She picks up the plates and blushes as she catches my eye. "Hello again, Mr. Hough."

I chuckle, "If Dad is 'Carl,' I think you can call me Marcus."

She blushes even more. "Yes, sir." She saunters over to Kevin and hands him a plate.

I watch her profile as she takes a bite of apple fritter, and then she turns to suck the icing from her fingers while she locks eyes with me. She turns bright red, but she doesn't turn away. I wink at her and turn back to Dad.

"How is the farm sale going, son?" Dad asks.

"I close on Thursday," I tell him. "The money will be available in your account Friday morning."

Dad clarifies, "I won't have access to it directly. You control it, right?"

I nod, "That's right, Dad. I have the Power of Attorney. I wonder if I should put it in a trust for you. I'll talk to the lawyer about it."

"Whatever," Dad says. "I supposedly have promised thousands of dollars and cars to staff and residents. It's probably best if I don't have access to it."

I nod, "Anytime you want to do something, talk it through with me. We will agree together on what to do."

Dad nods and pats my hand. "Sounds good, Son."

While we enjoy sweet, yeasty treats, we visit about all the latest gossip from the residents, what he's learned from the farmer grapevine, and interesting things he's seen looking out the window toward the highway.

Dad starts yawning, so I drain my coffee and wheel him back to his room. Kevin walks in. "Do you need to go to the bathroom first, Carl?"

"Yeah," Dad responds. "I'll talk to you tomorrow, son."

"Okay. Love you, Dad"

"Yep," Dad says. That's about as emotive as my dad ever goes. I smile and kiss his forehead.

I tell Kevin goodbye and head out to the truck.

After having the donuts, I really don't need lunch, but maybe some protein or a salad would be a good balance. I stop by the bank on the way back to the farm to pick up one thousand in hundreds, plus forty dollars in fives and ones for Dad. I eat some left-overs from last night's dinner, and text Denise with 'Honey check!'

She sends back, '*In love with Sir. Very busy. Kinda sore. CU this PM. XOXO.*'

I smile as I finish lunch. I fill four water bottles, pee, and drive to Scranton.

Thirty minutes later, I park in front of a machine shed outside Scranton, Kansas. I tuck Denise's pistol into my belt behind my back before I exited the truck.

A fit man that appears to be in his mid-sixties walks out of the people door of the shed. He has very thin hair and dark-rimmed glasses on a round face. He's holding a tan Bull Mastiff on a short leash. The dog and man are equally quiet and intense.

I say, "Hello. I'm Marcus Hough here to see Martin Greenbaum."

"Zeus, jump," the gentleman says. The dog lays down like his legs were chopped out from under him. The man pats the dog's head and unsnaps the leash from its collar. He steps forward and offers his hand. "I'm Martin Greenbaum. Welcome, Mr. Hough."

"Please call me Marcus, sir." I clasp his firm grip as we share a single firm shake.

"Okay, Marcus. Step inside and let us discuss your needs." He waves me toward the door.

Inside are a variety of locked, heavy-duty cages with weapons, parts, and supplies. There are tons of metal and woodworking machines. There are gun safes all along two of the walls.

Martin officers me a cup of coffee and waves me to a stool next to his bench. I accept the coffee and sit on the edge of the stool.

I give Mr. Greenbaum a synopsis of recent events and the perceived threats - the highlights from Daniel's attack to the recent attack by his brothers.

Mr. Greenbaum asks about any training I might have in firearms and personal defense. I share my history shooting as a kid, my time in the military, and my different martial arts training experiences. I also tell him that my girlfriend used to be a trap and skeet competitor and has a concealed carry permit.

I finish by telling him, "Mr. Greenbaum, I am looking to protect my home, my people, and my property. I think I need home defense weapons, concealed carry weapons, and gun safes for vehicles. I definitely need advice."

Greenbaum says, "Guns are good for home and personal defense, but don't forget other weapons. Bow, crossbow, knives, batons, even dart guns and slingshots are all useful in certain circumstances. All are also less likely to cause prejudice in a jury than a military style weapon."

I nod, and he pulls a pistol and brings it to bear as though he intends to shoot me. I toss the remnants of my coffee in his face, slap the gun hand away from me, and do an overhand twisting disarm.

I drop the magazine on the pistol to find it is empty. I open the chamber to find no round in it.

Greenbaum says, "Damn! I expected you to freeze or run. I figured there was maybe a ten percent chance you'd try to hit me. Coffee? Nope, I didn't see that one coming."

I set the empty gun on the bench and hand him my handkerchief. He waves it away with a chuckle as he pulls his own from his pocket. "You've got a good start, Marcus."

He wipes his face and polishes his glasses before getting up off his stool. "Come." He leads me over to a gun safe and opens it. Inside are a variety of shotguns that are what I would consider tactical configurations.

He picks something that looks like a sawed-off shotgun. Greenbaum says, "If you're going to use a shotgun, you might as well go 12-gauge. Even a .410 has a psychological effect and can be lethal, but a 12-gauge has nearly guaranteed stopping power inside thirty-to-forty feet - assuming you use the right ammo. This little fellow is nice because it's short enough to maneuver in a house. This is a Mossberg 590 Shockwave 12-gauge pump. This particular model is called the 'nightstick.' There is another model that has a 10-round magazine, but this one only holds five in the tube magazine, plus one in the chamber."

"I didn't know shotguns had magazines," I admit.

"They can; although, this weapon is not legally classified as a shotgun. That's how they can sell it with this pistol grip and a fourteen-inch barrel with no special license. It's perfect for inside a house. The magazine-fed model is an inch longer but still compact enough for in the house. The cons are that federal laws do not classify it as a shotgun, so the standard rules about barrel length *etcetera* don't apply. As a result of the lack of clear classification from the feds, state and local law enforcement can make decisions on a whim whether it's legal or not. Also, it's harder to control since it doesn't have a shoulder stock, and it does have a shorter barrel."

Mr. Greenbaum picks up a standard shotgun. "This is the Benelli M4. It's generally viewed as either the number one or two choice for a semi-auto tactical shotgun. Honestly, you could buy two good tactical pump shotguns for the price of this one. It is, however, a great weapon."

"Oka-a-a-ay," I respond skeptically. "I was thinking I wanted a nine-mil and a shotgun."

Greenbaum looks at me for a moment. "I would say get the Shockwave. Keep it in your house, put it in the toolbox of your truck when you leave. Take this one, and I'll trade you full value on the magazine-fed one when I get it in if you want it. You can get better deals on nine-mils at any gun shop - cheaper than I can do unless you want something special. Getting ammo is key. With all the social unrest over the last few years, shops keep having runs on ammo. The Gun Garage in north Topeka tends to keep plenty in stock. I have connections if they can't get what you need. Keep at least five hundred rounds of nine-mil, and a couple hundred 12-gauge on hand. You'll want to put at least one thousand rounds through each weapon to get your skills sharp."

"Okay," I agree. "Anything else?"

"Yes. Get a bow and learn how to use it. Get a dog or two - big ones with strong protective instincts. Bull Mastiffs and Rottweilers are good choices. Keep up your martial arts study. Maybe take some intensive self-defense training. Agile Tactical out of Topeka is nationally known," he says.

I gawp at him, and he grins. "You look a little overwhelmed, Marcus."

"I'm just trying to figure out how to make a living and take care of my family while doing all this," I tell him.

He laughs. "Take your time. Get the weapons and learn how to fire them. I can install safes in your vehicles for pistols. Get dogs in the next few months. Do the rest over the next couple of years."

I sigh and smile ruefully. "Sounds good. Any idea where I can get dogs?"

"I know some people - breeders and trainers. Let me ask around," Mr. Greenbaum says. "I have a preference for Mastiffs, but Rottweilers are also a good breed for family dogs and guard dogs. Do you have a preference?"

"No. I always had mutts growing up. Mostly German Shepherd and Lab mixes. I was thinking about getting a dog anyway, so that one isn't much of a stretch," I tell him.

Mr. Greenbaum says, "You should probably train with them. Learn their commands. Maybe work with an attack dummy. I can set that up, too."

"Your dog is a Mastiff, right?" I ask.

"Yep. He's great," Greenbaum says. "He's the third one I've had. Each was an excellent watchdog, attack dog, and family dog."

"I'll take the sawed-off, er...Mossberg Shockwave. I'll want a safe under the driver seat of that GMC outside and another for my girl-friend's SUV when it gets out of the shop. Let me know what you learn about dogs. Anything else?" I ask.

"Call me Martin," he says. "Five hundred for the shotgun, and I'll include a box of three-inch shells, double-aught buckshot. Payment on delivery when the safes come in. Same for anything really."

I pull out my wallet and extract five one-hundred-dollar bills and hand them over. I get a quick class on how to break down and the clean weapon. Martin pulls a box of shotgun shells from a metal wall locker that is packed with identical boxes. He promises to call me when he has the safes on hand and information on dogs.

I put the Shockwave and ammo in the toolbox in the bed of the pickup, wave to Martin, and drive back to the farm.

After pulling the truck into the garage, I run inside the house to start a mug of coffee before running out to the equipment shed.

I root around and find an old burlap seed bag. It's clean inside despite the dust on the outside of the sack. I shake it off, lock up the shed, and walk over to the pickup in the garage. I put the shotgun and the box of shells inside the gunny sack. The gunny sack goes back in the toolbox of the truck. I hurry inside to pee, grab my coffee mug, lock up the house, lock the toolbox, and back the truck out of the garage.

As I leave the driveway, I'm thinking maybe I should be backing into the garage. We always combat parked in the army, but the reason was you needed to be able to leave quickly in combat. Plus, you always had a ground guide in the army. I've always thought it was stupid when civilians do it, but I may have to reconsider given the recent attacks. A quick getaway could be critical. I pull onto the highway toward Topeka looking forward to seeing Denise soon.

After stopping for gas in Pauline, I make my way to Topeka Boulevard and then right on 10th Avenue. I find a spot fairly close to the entrance of the Supreme Court building. I check that Denise's pistol is in position at my back and that my jean jacket falls over it before walking to the building entrance.

I step inside the doors and see a small waiting area in front of a security station with metal detectors. The three cops on duty and the big guy in the waiting area all turn to look at me, but my attention is caught by Denise walking toward me. She is looking a little dewy in black yoga pants and lavender sports bra peeking out of a lavender tracksuit jacket. Her satchel is slung over her shoulder, and the tote bag she uses for her change of clothes is hooked over the same elbow. Her shiny auburn hair is pulled back into a short ponytail. She's sexy as hell, and I can't help but grin at her as my blood flows south.

Denise notices me and gives me a bright smile. She waves to the guards as she passes, "Until tomorrow, gentlemen." They are all obviously entranced with her, but she's oblivious as she launches into my waiting arms to collect a kiss. "Marc, I've missed you today."

"I've missed you too, Denise," I tell her honestly. "Shall I feed you, my lady?"

She grins as she says, "I love being your lady." She looks around and startles as she notices the big guy in the waiting area. I don't know him, but he looks familiar. He stands and stalks toward us. He's a little taller than my 6'3" height and probably half-again as heavy as I am. His presence screams 'cop' - solid round torso, muscled arms, wide shoulders, crew cut dark hair, square jaw, and a belligerent attitude. The guy has the biggest hands I've ever seen.

Denise steps behind me, and I feel her free hand snake under my jacket to grasp the pistol. "Seamus!" she exclaims. "What are you doing here?"

"I came for an accounting, Denise," he growls. He reeks of stale cigarette smoke. "One of my sons is dead, one is in a coma, and one is in jail. How did that happen?" I see him cut off the 'bitch' he was about to use to punctuate the question.

I decide it's time for me to join the conversation. "That's really easy, Seamus. You failed to raise your boys, so they thought they could run around and act like wild animals."

"Who the fuck are you?" he growls at me.

"Marcus Hough. You?" I ask despite having picked it up from context.

"I'm Seamus Connolly, Police Chief of Salina, Kansas, and father to the men you assaulted," he yells at me.

"Assaulted?" I ask quietly. "One of them pounded on the door and yelled 'open the door, Denise, you bitch' before he started blindly shooting through the door. When he broke in, I killed him with a closet pole. When your elder sons decided they were going to beat me to a pulp with a sledgehammer and shovel before...how did Joseph say it? Oh yes, he was going to 'butcher me like a hog.' He claimed to have done that multiple times, so I believed him. I countered their attacks, disarmed them, and cuffed them rather than killing them. You should thank me for not killing them too."

He opens his mouth to speak, and I hold up a hand to interrupt him. I'm careful not to step closer as I tell him, "But wait, Seamus. It gets better. The oldest one attacked the deputy that took him to the hospital to get his broken arm set. Then he killed an orderly in the hospital parking lot and attacked a Topeka policeman in an attempt to kill the woman your boys beat nearly to death to get my name and address. Other policemen chased him away, and fortunately, I was able to apprehend him again. It's unfortunate that I crushed his larynx and cracked his skull in the process. Are you picking up on the theme here,

Seamus? Your boys are all undisciplined thugs with no regard for the law or human life. Where did they learn that? They are unworthy to wear a badge because they are CRIMINALS!"

The big man pokes a sausage-sized finger into my chest. I reach behind me and push Denise towards the guards. She takes the pistol with her and stands next to the guard with the pistol held behind her thigh out of sight.

"You're gonna pay, you sonofabitch," Seamus growls as he pokes my chest again. I step back now that Denise is clear. Seamus has another idea.

The big cop grabs my shirt front with his right hand as he fires a left hook at me. I'm able to deflect it with my right hand as my left comes over his grabbing hand to again deflect the punch - this time past my head and down to pin his other hand. As I pin his arms, I thrust the palm of my right hand into his nose and then circle the same hand to hammer the base of my fist into his left temple before I step up the line to my right and slam the edge of my palm into the hinge of his jaw.

I roll the big guy as he drops to the ground so that he lands face down onto his abused face. He doesn't make a sound. I fold his left arm behind his back and kneel on it.

One of the cops on guard duty rushes over and cuffs him. I tell him, "Thanks. He's probably carrying. All three of his sons were when they attacked us." I back up and Denise hurries forward to hug me. She surreptitiously hands me the pistol, and I holster it as nonchalantly as possible.

"We ran him through the metal detector when he arrived because he looked disreputable. The dumbshit tried to pull rank on us. We got two pistols, a knife, a baton, and brass knuckles off him. That probably didn't help his attitude any," the officer says.

He stands and looks me square in the eye. "We were about to have you do the same."

I smile and admit, "You would have gotten Denise's pistol and my pocket knife." He glares at me.

Denise gives him puppy-dog eyes. "Marcus doesn't own a pistol, and I didn't want him running around unarmed with the Connollys attacking us so frequently. We are about to go to get him his own, and I'll be locking mine here with you gentlemen again tomorrow."

"The Chief Justice and the Bailiff both signed off on it. You're allowed to keep yours with you, Ms. Schneider," the officer tells her with a sigh.

"Do you need statements from us, Officer?" I ask.

"Just your contact information. Three officers and at least two cameras witnessed the altercation," he says.

Another cop waves me over and takes my information from my new Kansas driver's license. He notes the address and my phone number, too.

Denise and I wish the officers well as we leave. Seamus is just starting to stir and moan. I don't envy the officers having to deal with that asshole.

As we walk to the truck, I hold Denise close. "I see you made yoga class today, Pet. I'm proud of you."

"Thank you, Sir. No panties under my yoga tights, Sir," she says with a smirk. I squeeze her firm ass, and she leans into me. She looks up at me, "We need to stop by the hospital before we go to the range. They brought Aliyah out of her coma this afternoon. She's asking for me. Maybe we can grab something to eat quickly in between."

"Yes, Love. We need to console her. She took a beating for us," I agree grimly.

We drive to Stormont-Vail hospital and park in front, by the North Tower entrance. I smile and point at the library across 10th Avenue where Denise and I met. I'll always have a fondness for that place. Denise grins at me and says, "One of my favorite places in town."

I wink at her. "I can't imagine why."

She hooks my arm and looks up at me. "Well, Sir. Let me explain. Before I met Sir, I would go there to get smutty romance novels to help me approximate a sex life. And then one day, Sir met me there and led me off to a life of love and sexual fulfillment I could never have imagined."

She kisses me passionately before murmuring. "The hem of my tights is giving me quite the camel toe. It's making me excited, Sir."

I offer, "I could fuck you right here in the parking lot, Pet."

She gives me a gentle frown. "That sounds delightful, Marc. Sadly, my friend needs me. Shall we?"

She leads me to the information desk, and we learn they moved Aliyah to a standard ward. We take the elevator to the sixth floor and find her room. We walk in to find Liyana Sadduzai sitting in a chair next to a bed, holding the hand of a slender, bruised woman with bandages on her face.

"Ah," Aliyah's mother says quietly. "She's been asking for you, Denise."

The figure on the bed moans, "Duh - neeeesssss."

Denise gasps and approaches the bed swiftly. "Aliyah! Oh, you poor baby. I'm sorry we put you through this."

"Nah yur fau," the broken woman mutters. I interpret that as 'not your fault.' The one eye I can see is locked on Denise's face, glistening with tears. The other is covered by bandages. She seems very slender, almost waifish. Both of her hands are wrapped, the left in a cast and right in bandages.

Denise waives me forward. "Aliyah, this is Marcus. He caught them. They will rot in jail for what they did to you."

"Hello, Aliyah," I say over Denise's shoulder. "I'm sorry they did this to you. If there is anything we can do to help, please let us know."

"Kee Deneess saa," she mutters.

"Keep Denise safe?" I ask. She nods minutely before turning her attention back to Denise momentarily. "I will, Aliyah. To my last breath." She looks at me steadily for a moment before giving another minute nod and turning her attention back to Denise.

Denise says, "I talked to the prosecutor today. They've been charged with three counts of attempted murder. One is here under guard due to injuries from when Marcus stopped him."

Aliyah looks at me with her single warm, dark, bloodshot eye. "Tha oo Mar ksss," she manages.

"You're welcome, Aliyah. Seriously, anything," I tell her. I caress Denise's back. "Honey, we should probably let her rest."

"Nooooo," Aliyah moans. "Plee stay."

"For a little while, Love," Denise responds. "Marcus and I need to go take care of some things in a little bit, but we can stay for a few minutes." She holds her friend's right hand. I back off and lean against the door. Eventually, Aliyah falls asleep, so Denise and I take our leave after collecting hugs from her mother. Liyana Sadduzai follows us into the corridor and wraps an arm around each of us.

Liyana says, "She is going into surgery in a couple of days to repair her cheekbone and orbital. I'm afraid she will have permanent damage to her eye, but we have hope she will recover."

I tell her, "I don't pray often, but I'll make an exception in this case."

"Me, too," Denise adds. She kisses Liyana's cheek, and we walk back to the truck.

6

ARMING OURSELVES

Denise is fairly quiet during the drive to the range. We backtrack to Topeka Boulevard and drive north to cross the river. We turn east on State Highway 24, staying on the access road until we turn south again on Meridien road to arrive at the Gun Garage.

I return Denise's pistol to her before we exit the truck, and retrieve my Mossberg gunny sack from the toolbox. I pull out the box of shells and leave them in the toolbox. I relock the toolbox and follow Denise into the shop.

We clear our weapons at a barrel similar to the ones I'm familiar with from my time in the army. I retrieve my six shells from the sand, blow the sand off them, and put them in my pocket. We stop at the counter and register our weapons at the desk. Denise is greeted by a pretty, caramel-skinned, tall, lean, black woman with curls tight against her skull.

The woman says, "Hi, Denise. Is this the man you were gushing about?"

"Hello, Karen," Denise says, embracing the woman lightly. "Yes, this is Marcus."

She looks at the Shockwave on the counter and cocks an eyebrow.

She grins at me. "Hello, Marcus. I'm Karen Murdock. Welcome to Gun Garage."

I clasp her hand. "Hello, Karen. Marcus Hough. It's a pleasure. We need to do some shopping and then spend some time on the range. I haven't been to a range for several years, so you might want to watch me."

Karen chuckles, "I'll get you started, but this one...," she points at Denise, "...can teach the range safety classes. She'll keep you honest."

Denise waves a hand in dismissal.

"So," Karen starts, "Tell me what you're looking for."

I collect my thoughts. "A couple of automatic pistols. I fired the Beretta M9 when I was in the army, so I'm comfortable with that despite not being impressed with their quality. However, I'd like a weapon for concealed carry, too. I like the nine-mil, but a .45 would be okay too. Nine-mil would make logistics of ammunition simpler since Denise also uses it."

Karen nods, so I continue. "I think a magazine-fed shotgun in 12-gauge. Same shells as that one," pointing to the Shockwave. "Preferably semi-auto rather than a pump, but either will be fine." She purses her lips and nods. I continue, "Finally, I'd like an AR-15 or AR-10. I was consistently accurate with an M-16 out to 300 meters, so an AR-15 is probably fine."

Karen says, "Yeah, ammo choice can make a difference, but essentially if you use the right rounds, there's not a lot of difference between the drift and drop between the AR-15 and an AR-10 at that range. There are plenty of guys with religion that will argue, but most of the high-end scopes treat them the same."

Karen takes us around the shop, and we fill a cart with weapons and accessories to try out. Karen then escorts us to the range. She snarks as we approach our stations in the range, "You better buy some of these because I have to clean any of the ones you don't buy."

"If I make a mess, I clean it up," I tell her.

She grins and says to Denise, "I think you got a winner there, Denise. If you throw him back, let me know."

Denise grins, "He cooks and keeps his own house. I moved in and am getting SERIOUSLY spoiled."

"Introduce me to his brother," Karen quips back. Denise looks flustered for a moment, but I just shake my head gently and smile. I'm rewarded with an incandescent smile from my lady.

We end up making Karen quite happy. I end up buying an M&P M2 compact nine-mil and a used Glock 17 with clip-on holsters and a shoulder rig for each. Denise gets a Benelli M4 shotgun, but she likes the M&P so much that she gets one of those, too. Remembering what Martin said, I look at some less-expensive options for shotguns.

For shotguns, I consider both the Mossberg 930 Tactical SPX, an Armscor VR80, and a Panzer BP-12 GEN 2 Bullpup. Both the VR80 and the Bullpup were used, but pristine. I liked the Mossberg but ended up getting the VR80 as it is magazine fed. Spare magazines I know how to deal with. Pushing shells into a tube is new. Karen mentioned there is a 'Sidewinder' adapter for the Mossberg that attaches a magazine, but I'm not very comfortable with that idea. Denise and I each get a Ruger SR22 to use for basic marksmanship practice - the .22 LR shells are much cheaper than 9mm. Denise gets an XT3, semi-auto .410 shotgun for the same reason. I decide to pass on the AR-15 for now, but I do like the Ruger Mini-14 as an alternative option for the future.

Karen has me put an adapter onto my Shockwave to fire mini shells - the Opsol Mini Clip. The mini-shells are amazing! The shells still have plenty of stopping power for up-close with slugs and double-aught buckshot, a lot less recoil, plus it gives me two more rounds of capacity. They are great for practicing and would probably work in the house, too.

I buy the weapons and two hundred rounds of mini-shells, two hundred rounds of 2 3/4" 12-gauge, and two hundred rounds of nine-mil - store policy is no more than two hundred of any round except .22 caliber. I get a block of 500 .22 LR cartridges for the Ruger and my dad's rifle, plus cleaning supplies.

Denise pays for her weapons and ammo, and we fill out all the required paperwork. Kansas' gun laws are pretty permissive, but I still have to submit to a federal background check. Denise and I clean the weapons we fired while Karen is working on that. She explains that Kansas allows both open and concealed carry without any issues.

Despite having a new license, I am able to walk out with my purchases about thirty minutes after paying.

At the truck I load the M&P and clip it to my belt. Everything else goes in the 'back seat' - more like a cargo bench - in the cab of the truck.

As I pull out of the parking lot, Denise starts laughing. "You think we might be a little paranoid? I think I just turned into a prepper."

I chuckle mirthlessly. "I don't know how many more Connollys there are or who else Seamus might bring into this. He's still breathing, so I suspect he's not done yet."

Denise turns serious. "Yeah. There's one more you haven't met. I've only met him once - at the wedding. His name is Michael. Daniel always called him Mick. He left to join the Hays police after a couple of years at Salina. Daniel said he has an even bigger ego than Seamus."

"Hard to imagine," I observe with a frown. "How's Sonic sound for dinner? A coney dog and shake sound like plenty for me."

"Maybe just the shake," Denise says. I look over at her, and she grabs my hand with a slight smile.

She directs me to the nearest Sonic, and then we make our way home.

We get home and start a weapon cleaning party while we hydrate. A couple of hours later we put the weapons away. The longer guns go in the closet, the Shockwave goes under my side of the bed, and the M&P pistols go into our nightstands.

Denise and I sit in the living room on the couch for a drink to unwind before bed. She says, "Marc, something is bothering me."

"What's that, Pet?"

Denise chews on her lip for a moment and leans against my chest. She speaks when she's ready. "When Aliyah interviewed me for the newspaper article, I noticed this strange expression on her face as I was getting ready to leave. I've seen her do it before and never thought anything of it, but this time it reminded me of something."

"What's that, my love?" I prod.

She pauses for a moment and then sighs. "It is similar to the way I look in the mirror when I'm daydreaming about you." She shifts to look up at me. "Is it possible for her to be in love with me?"

I nod. "Certainly it is. It's not unheard of," I answer as I look down in her eyes.

"But she's Muslim," Denise says. "It's against their faith."

I shrug, "Christianity is only slowly coming to accept homosexuality. Many devout Christians would still argue it's sinful." Denise takes a sip of wine and burrows into my chest. I ask, "What do you think about that?"

"I don't know," Denise whispers. The hand she has wrapped under my shoulder plays with my hair. "She's my best friend - has been for nearly eight years. We met at Washburn my first year of law school in an aerobics class and hit it off. She was my Maid of Honor when I married Daniel despite not liking him. She held me and dried my tears when I discovered he'd cheated on me and all through the divorce. We make a point to get together at least once a week - usually dinner at each other's houses. During the time of my divorce, we were together nearly every evening. Since you and I met, it's been lunches."

"You can spend more time with her, honey. I won't be hurt or jealous of you spending time with her," I tell her.

"You are definitely not Daniel," she says as she squeezes me tighter. "He used to bitch about me having her over, going to her house, or even talking to her on the phone. He would say, 'You should drop that raghead like a hot potato.' He was such a disgusting pig."

"My limited experience with him supports your opinion," I agree with a grimace. "She's just gone through an emotional experience, Denise. She's going to need you to be there for her."

Denise whispers, "What if she makes a pass at me?"

"How does it feel when you think about it?" I ask.

"Kinda weird. Scary," Denise whispers. "Exciting."

I nod and say, "This might be a good time for me to talk about Toni for a moment."

Denise looks up at me with a puzzled expression. I smirk slightly before continuing. "Toni had a girlfriend - Lynette Colbert. She was the volleyball coach and advanced math teacher at the school where Toni taught. They had a relationship much like what you and Aliyah have. When we learned that I was going to Afghanistan, Toni said she wanted to take Lynette as a lover while I was deployed."

"Really?" Denise barely avoids spilling her wine as she sits up suddenly.

"Yep," I say eloquently. "Toni said she loved Lynette very similar to how she loved me. She wanted to try it. Lynnette was bi and had just broken up with her partner of five years at the time. She had been over to the house a lot for the same kind of emotional support Aliyah gave you. Toni said she had a girlfriend for a short time in high school before she met me, and never got beyond kissing and petting. We talked about it, and I stewed over it for several days. Toni said she wouldn't do it if I didn't support her in it. I still struggled. Toni and I watched a fair amount of Lesbian romances and porn for two weeks. Despite the contrived relationships in the videos, I came to the conclusion that relationships between women are different than a heterosexual relationship - even if the woman loves the man very much."

I sip my beer, and Denise asked, "So what happened?"

"Well, I eventually agreed to Toni's request. Two weeks before I left for Afghanistan, we invited Lynette over for dinner. After dinner, as we were relaxing on the couch, Toni got up, cupped Lynette's face, and kissed her. After the kiss broke, Toni said 'I've been wanting to do that for some time.' Lynette looked at me. I told her, 'I'm going to be gone to Afghanistan for nine-to-twelve months. Toni is going to need your friendship and comfort. She wants to be your lover. You have my blessing.' When I got back, they both greeted me when I landed and both of them kissed me. After that, Lynette would join Toni and me once or twice a week - Lynette and I would both pleasure Toni. If it wasn't volleyball season, they would frequently go to Lynette's house after school. During the volleyball season, Toni would spend an evening with Lynette on her own, but she always came home to sleep with me."

Denise looks at me puzzled, "So you and Lynette were lovers, too?"

I grimace. "Not so much. We kissed, caressed, and hugged, but honestly, we were both deeply in love with Toni." I sip my beer before I reveal the last bit. "When I told you I went on one date before moving back?" Denise nods. "It was Lynette. It just felt wrong for both of us without Toni. It was like her ghost was there the whole time. I told Lynette 'I'm sorry,' held her as we both cried, and then I kissed her goodbye."

"It sounds like Toni had you both wrapped around her finger," Denise observes. "I think I would be quite upset about how she treated both of you if she were alive."

I chuckle and kiss Denise lovingly. "Pet, as with most of the trouble in my relationship with Toni, I made a mistake. Lynette was sexy and athletic. I found her very attractive, but I let Toni become the pivot. Toni would have gladly shared Lynette with me, but I was afraid of ruining my relationship with Toni. So instead of safeguarding our relationship, I set Lynette and myself both up for pain and loneliness when Toni died." I kiss Denise again. "However, that set up my departure from Flagstaff, so I could meet you. I gotta say, I have no regrets since I met you."

Denise kisses me. She stares into my eyes, "I kissed a girl once - freshman year of college. We were both curious and a little drunk. We kissed. I pulled off my shirt. She loved my breasts."

"So do I."

"I know," she says with a knowing grin. "Would you like to scrub them clean? I'm still all sweaty from yoga."

"Let's go," I tell her before draining my beer. I set the beer glass aside as Denise stands to drain her glass. I stand and wrap my arms around her.

She holds up her empty wine glass, "Please, Sir."

I take the glass from her and set it beside mine on the side table before I kiss her deeply. I fill my hands with her amazing ass and lift Denise into the air. She wraps her long legs around my waist and arms around my neck as I carry her back to the bedroom.

I set Denise on her feet and tell her, "Hands in the air, Pet."

Denise grins at me and raises her hands high above her head. I grab the hem of her sports bra and ease it up over her magnificent breasts. I work the tight, stretchy garment over her shoulders and head. As the garment reveals her eyes, I notice they are sparkling with joy and lust.

Denise's arms slowly settle around my neck before she leans in to collect another kiss. I cup her heavy mammaries and squeeze them gently, and Denise moans into my mouth. I hook my thumbs into the waistband of her tights, and she shimmies her hips provocatively as I push the tights past her hips. I kneel down and kiss Denise's landing strip as I push the garment down her legs. I kiss farther down her mons and down her thighs as her tights reach her ankles.

Denise pulls my face into her mons and holds me tight for balance. She lifts her right leg, and I slide her pants off her foot. She switches which foot is in the air, and I slide the garment off her other foot as I inhale the scent of her arousal.

I slide my hands up Denise's strong, shapely legs to cup her glorious ass, holding her in place while I tongue her clitoris.

Denise moans, "God in heaven! I love you so much, Sir! I surrender! I give you all that I am!"

I kiss my way up her abdomen, suckle each already hard nipple briefly, kiss up her décolletage, up her neck, and up her jaw to capture her mouth.

Denise's nimble fingers unbuckle my belt, unbutton my jeans, and push them and my boxers down to my hips. I shimmy to get them to drop while Denise continues to kiss me and unbutton my shirt.

"Sir," she gasps as she pushes my shirt off my shoulders. "You've never fucked me in the shower!" She pulls my shirt off as I step on the hem of my jeans and pull my legs out one at a time.

I gasp, "Let's fix that, Pet."

I take Denise's hand and lead her into the master bath. She detours to relieve her bladder as I get the shower started. I take her place at the loo as we wait for the water to warm. Denise is removing her makeup at the sink when I step up next to her to wash my fingers.

She says, "I've been using less war paint since we started dating - the night at Chez Yasu."

"I noticed," I admit as she finishes. "I like it. It lets your natural beauty shine through more." I caress her ass before leading her into the shower by the hand she offers me. We hold each other and rotate under the shower until we're both wet. I murmur in her ear, "If we started dating the night of Chez Yasu, what was I to you before?"

Denise pulls my chin around to look into my eyes guilelessly. "My savior. The beautiful man that saved me from my desperate, cold, loneliness," she replies.

I capture her lips and press her to the back of the shower enclosure. Denise lifts one leg and curls it around my left hip. I hold her asscheek in my hand as I slot myself in her entrance. I press forward into her moist, hot depths as she moans into my mouth. I caress her face as I kiss her. I feel her left leg curling around my hip so I can drive deeper into her.

I release Denise's face and hook my right arm under her left knee before grabbing her left buttock. Then I reposition my left arm to mirror the right - all while devouring Denise's mouth. I start to drive my hips harder.

Denise whimpers into my mouth and her nails dig into the flesh of my back as she holds me close. We say nothing as I fuck my beautiful love against the wall with the water beating out a gentle tattoo on our flesh. We kiss ravenously, break to stare deeply into each other's eyes as we thrust our hips hungrily into each other, and then kiss ravenously again. Denise starts to keen softly into my mouth as her body starts to tremble.

I'm getting close myself. I massage her rear sphincter gently as I continue to fuck her. That tips her over the edge. Her whole body spasms outward from the tight ridged muscles she's clamping around my cock. The additional flood of fluid in Denise's channel eases my effort as I get more frenzied as well.

Denise releases my mouth to suck in gasping breaths. I suckle her neck as my own bliss approaches. Denise's breath had started to slow, but the pace is picking up quickly again. Her body vibrates in my arms before she clenches hard around me. I follow her orgasm quickly with one of my own as I struggle not to slip down to the shower floor.

Once I've come back to my own mind, I slowly release Denise's right leg. She nods, so I let the other down.

Denise lays her head on my chest and squeezes me. "Purrrrrfect," she murmurs.

"Yes, you are," I respond.

We slowly start sudsing each other. We take our time, relishing each moment spent caressing each other's flesh. In the back of my mind I know there are things that are still dangerous in our life, but I can't think about them now. Now, I just relish being with Denise and our growing connection.

The shower begins to cool, so we get serious about rinsing off. I squeegee the shower while Denise towels off.

She says, "I need to dry my hair. If I go to bed with it wet, it will look like a mop in the morning. If I dry it, at least it will look okay pinned up or in a ponytail."

"Okay, Pet." I kiss her shoulder, before I pick up the discarded clothing. I empty all the pockets. Denise has some lip balm, a tissue, a golf pencil, and a folded piece of paper with a to-do list on it in her jacket pocket. I set those on her nightstand and put all of the soiled clothing in the hamper. It looks like I've got a full load collected, so I start the washer before returning to the bedroom.

Denise is lowering a short cotton gown over her body. The hemline is higher than mid-thigh, long sleeves with a ruffle on the cuff, and an open collar on the bodice held together loosely with a string that is not tied. She holds her arms out to her sides. "It's called a 'poet's shirt.' Do you like it?"

"You look sexy as hell, Denise. Just like always. You do have a gift for selecting clothing that really accentuates the gifts God gave you," I answer as I walk toward her with my rising cock leading the way.

My little friend slides under the hemline of her gown as her arms encircle my neck. "I think it might be nice to have my shoulders covered at night since it's getting colder."

"All good, Love. I'm bushed. Are you ready to sleep?" I ask.

She nods. I release her to set her alarm on her phone. I do the same, ensure the pistol is where I can easily get to it in the nightstand, and crawl under the covers. Denise joins me, and I turn out the light. I spoon around Denise as she lays on her side and quickly begin to drop off.

Denise asks out of the blue, "Marc, what do I do if Aliyah makes a pass at me, or tells me she is in love with me?"

I squeeze her gently. "Listen to your heart," I respond sleepily. "It knows the right thing to do."

I drift off as Denise kisses my hand and squirms back to cuddle closer.

❦   7   ❦

MEETING ALIYAH

I wake up, and the house is dark. I'm lying on my right side, and I feel Denise's breath on the back of my neck. Her arm is wrapped around me, resting about half-way between my navel and my pubic bone.

I check the time on my phone. My alarm is going to go off in about twenty minutes. Denise fusses and rolls over. I follow her and kiss her cheek gently. She smiles and mutters in her sleep. I try to gently crawl off the bed without disturbing her. I shut off my alarm and take a leak before pulling on some sweats and tucking my feet into some slippers. I grab my phone and my pistol, and head to the living room. I do some yoga stretches on the carpet for about twenty minutes - essentially a sunrise salute plus - and then start preparing breakfast in the kitchen.

I decide on the menu, so I start making spinach-boursin omelettes, bacon, and wheat toast with butter.

As I'm throwing the sauteed spinach in a little bacon fat in a small skillet, Denise walks in wearing slippers and her poet's shirt. She wraps her arms around me and lays her chin on my shoulder.

"You got an early start this morning," Denise observes.

"Not that much. I woke up twenty minutes before my alarm went off," I tell her. "I invested the time in some yoga stretches."

"Hmmm. You should have had me do it with you," she says as she rubs her face on my shoulder.

I chuckle. "You would probably laugh your butt off watching me do yoga. I did all the yoga I know and it took me a whole twenty minutes."

"I could teach you. I managed to get certified during my undergrad time, and I've kept it current," she says. "Maybe you could teach me karate in return."

I frown slightly at the thought. "I'd probably teach you something else, or a combination of skills and tactics from a variety of arts. Learning karate is good for self-defense, but it's not necessarily the quick path. I'll need to think about how best to get you ready quickly."

"Think about it, Marc. Against large male attackers I would still be at a disadvantage, but some skill and training could only help," she says. She squeezes me and tickles my ribs. "Besides, I have this fantasy about you sparring with me, throwing me to the ground, and fucking me senseless on the mat."

I laugh out loud at that one. "That can be arranged regardless, Pet."

Denise kisses my neck and walks away. She says, "Gotta get ready for work."

I call out, "You okay with me going to class tonight?"

"Sure," I hear echo down the hall. "I should visit Aliyah this evening anyway. Maybe you can drop by after class."

"I will unless they decide to push us to exhaustion in class," I call back. I mutter to myself as I work at the stove. "I suppose I should get to know my girlfriend's other love interest."

"Not exactly the verbiage I was going to use, but I agree with the sentiment." I turn to see Denise leaning against the doorway from the hall to the dining room with a smirk on her face.

"We owe her for taking a beating for us," I point out.

"That too," Denise agrees as she returns to the kitchen to wrap her arms around me. "I bet she feels as much or more guilty about spilling the beans as you do about her being attacked."

"She shouldn't. Even people trained to resist torture will eventually cave," I tell Denise. "It's more of a question of when and how much misdirection they have the presence of mind to interject. I set down the spatula and turn to wrap my arms around my lover.

Denise presses her pointed globes into my chest as we kiss. I reach down to lift the hem of her gown to squeeze her firm, bare buttocks. She moans in my mouth. I start kissing down her jaw to her neck. I murmur, "If you don't get dressed, I'll tie you to the bed and fuck you all day long."

"Promises, promises," she gasps. She reaches down to remove my hands from her ass and backs away. "You are a very distracting man, Mr. Hough." She spins and sashays through the dining room to the hallway. I watch her grin over her shoulder as her sexy ass and legs disappear.

Denise calls out, "I love you, Sir!"

I laugh. "I love you too, Pet!"

Denise returns dressed in sensible pumps, a grey skirt, and a cream colored silk wrap-around blouse that emphasizes her beautiful breasts and narrow waist.

I sing as I carry the plates to the table. "I've got it bad, got it bad, got it bad...I'm hot for teacher."

Denise giggles as lays her blazer over the back of her chair and takes a seat. "Teacher, huh? A little role-play in our future, Sir?"

I laugh as I pour her a cup of coffee. "Could be, Pet."

She says, "Marc, you're spoiling me rotten. I can grab a breakfast burrito or sandwich from the cafeteria at work."

"I'll probably get lazy about it over time, but I am enjoying pampering you at the moment, Denise."

We eat and chat about our plans for the day. I rinse off the plates, and Denise loads them into the dishwasher. I fill her a mug to go while she clears and function checks her pistol. She loads it, chambers a round, and holsters it before clipping it onto her skirt. She grabs her valise and jacket, and I walk her out to her rental. I drop down to the ground and look under it with a flashlight for any signs of tampering. She gets in, pops the hood, and I check the engine compartment. Everything looks good, so I close the hood. I lean in to kiss Denise in the early morning light. She smiles and backs out of the garage at 7:30.

I decide to check my truck too since I've already soiled my slippers and sweatpants on the dirty garage floor. I don't see any obvious issues, so I close the hood. I wipe off my slippers inside, grab my weapon, and return to the bedroom to dress for the day.

Forty-five minutes later, I'm parking the truck at the nursing home. Kelly, a plump, mid-thirties nurse greets me as I arrive and tells me Dad is still at breakfast. I grab a cup of coffee after giving Dad a hug. He's in the middle of visiting with several of the old farmers in his breakfast group. I pull up a chair and listen.

Eventually the old guys run out of gossip, so they ask about how I'm doing. I tell them I'm buying the farm from Dad, I'm planning to continue leasing to Rory McDonald, and my girlfriend has moved in. That leads to a bunch of questions about Denise. The two old gents from the Carbondale-Scranton-Overbrook area ask about 'that girl I ran off to chase' years ago. So I backtrack and explain that Toni and I got married, that she died a couple years ago, and so I moved up here to take care of Dad. I know I've told the story to them before, but I don't mind repeating it for them. They're nice old gents. After relating the Toni story, I tell them that I met Denise at the Topeka Library a few weeks back, and that we really hit it off.

I didn't plan to talk about the attacks, but Dad brought it up. Frank Albertson, my high-school shop teacher and a local farmer, said that he read the story in the Saturday paper. I ended up telling them about Daniel's attack, his brothers' attack, and my encounter with their father yesterday."

John Hesse, another old farmer from our church, said he had heard horrible stories about the police in Salina. He has family that lives out there, and he related that they all think of the Connolly family as the local mafia. One of John's sons works out there at the John Deere dealership.

Dad starts to yawn and says he's going to take a nap before sports time - balloon volleyball today. Sherry and Kevin show up to help the gents back to their rooms, and I head home to work.

I meditate with some yoga stretches and deep breathing before I check emails. I've got two other offers for editing jobs, so I accept them before jumping into the Buffalo Soldiers book. I work through lunch until about four o'clock with only short breaks for bathroom, stretching, and fluid replenishment.

At 4:00, I put the document down and log my time. I think I have only about three more hours left on Buffalo Soldiers. The guy's writing has improved as he's progressed through the book, so I'm picking up speed. I find fewer spelling and grammar issues; although, I mark it up for style a significant amount. There are still a significant number of passages that look like he's missing attributions. With any luck I'll finish it tomorrow.

I text Denise, and she calls me back. She sounds breathless, *"Just a short call, Marc. I wanted to hear your voice, but I'm late for yoga."*

"No problem, Sweetheart. I've been heads-down on the book I'm editing. I just wanted to let you know that I missed you," I tell her with a grin on her face.

"I miss you too. I've got another hour of work after yoga, and then I'm going to see Aliyah after work. Gotta run. Love you," she says quickly.

"Love you too, Denise. Bye." I barely got that last word out of my mouth before she disconnected.

I chuckle and start a skillet to cook a steak. I don't have any fresh vegetables left, but there's left-over spinach from this morning. I put on a small pot and cook up a cup of whole wheat penne to go with the rest of it - adding some red sauce from a jar after draining the pasta. I sit down and catch up on emails as I eat - lunch? dinner? linner? dunch? - my second meal of the day.

While I clean the kitchen, my mind turns to home defense. There is a security light on the equipment shed, but I think more motion-sensitive lights with phone alerts might be useful. A loud dog for an alarm, too. I like the idea of Mastiffs and Rottweilers, but I think they growl more than bark - I need to ask Martin.

I pull on my karate uniform - the white one that looks kinda grey-ish - and put the Shockwave under a towel covered by my street clothes. I'm about to leave when I get a text from Karen inviting me to a CCW class on Saturday and Sunday morning. I text Denise about it, and confirm with Karen to sign me up.

Karate class turns out to be very intense. I work bo-staff drills with the brown and black belts. I had to borrow a staff, because I no longer have one. The senior teacher in Topeka shows up for the class and leads the instruction. He is there frequently, but he travels between several classes around town so it's not a given he will be there any given night. We finish by sparring with foam-covered bo staffs. I do okay. I tag some opponents, and some tag me. Foam, or no foam, getting hit by a six-foot staff sucks. I lock my bag in a locker for a quick rinse in the shower before getting dressed and driving to Stormont-Vail hospital.

I grab a large bottle of water from the gift shop just before it closes, and I find Aliyah's room without any trouble. Aliyah is staring vacantly out the window and doesn't notice me standing in the door. The bandage over her eye is gone.

I knock gently, and the poor woman startles. "Would you like some company?" I ask.

"Marcus?" she asks.

"Yes," I say as I walk in. "My mom said that visits were the only thing good about being in the hospital, so I thought you might like a little company."

She waves to the chair, "Yes. Company would be nice. Would you hand me that scarf please?" She points to a long, wide, white scarf on the chair. Her speech is much more clear than yesterday. Her accent sounds English with a flavor of something else; it's lovely to listen to. Her long dark hair has been washed and brushed, and it glows in the low light. Her dark eyes watch me warily.

I pick the scarf up and hand it to her. She tries to wrap it around her face into a hijab. Despite the cast and splint on her arms, she manages to deftly get it in place.

I smile, "You made that look easy despite the casts."

She says dryly, "A lifetime of experience. Why have you come, Marcus? You don't know me at all."

I nod somberly and take the seat she offered, turning it to face her. "Aliyah, I don't know if you remember my comments from yesterday, but I meant every word. You took a beating for Denise and me. I owe you."

"Hardly," she says with disgust dripping from her voice. "I barely held back after they knocked me to the floor the first time."

"Hey," I lean forward and lay a hand on the splint of her right arm. "Everybody breaks, Aliyah. I told Denise this, even guys that are trained to resist eventually break despite what the movies would have you believe. You aren't trained for that, so there is no expectation that you hold out against those two bruisers. I fought them. I know they are big strong guys. You are positively waifish in comparison."

I see the pain in her eyes as tears start to flow. She snaps out a response, "I hate being a victim! I could do nothing against them! They have broken my body and permanently disfigured me! Do you see how the flesh below the left eyelid droops? I will be an ugly horror show for all my nieces and nephews forevermore."

"Aliyah you will never be ugly," I tell her. "You're a beautiful woman, and you will heal. Denise tells me you're a beautiful person in addition to being very pretty. I trust her judgment. The stories she told indicated you are a good friend. She loves you dearly."

Aliyah sobs, "She won't think that any longer. We argued, and I told her to leave."

"I will never leave you, Aliyah."

I turn to the door to see my beautiful lady standing in the doorway. She says, "Marc is right. I love you. You are the best friend I've ever had. I've seen other BFF relationships, and they aren't nearly as devoted or kind as you."

"So why are you planning to marry someone else?" the poor girl sobs.

"Because I love him, too. My love for him is very romantic and everything I've ever dreamed of. My love for you is true too, but I've never thought of you in a romantic way," Denise explains quietly. She grabs two tissues, giving one to Aliyah before sitting in my lap to dry her own eyes. I wrap an arm around her waist.

Denise continues, "I never experimented with girls. Well, other than a drunken party episode before I met you, which left us both pretty embarrassed later. You've never indicated any kind of interest in women, and I know that you have dated men."

Aliyah cries piteously. Denise and I both extend our hands to hold hers. Aliyah finally chokes out a response. "I cannot talk about this now." She looks from Denise to me and back to Denise.

"I can leave if you two need to talk," I offer.

"No," she whimpers. "I am an emotional mess right now, and I cannot have this conversation now regardless, Marcus." She reaches her cast across her body with a grimace to place her left hand over mine and Denise's. "You are both being kind and patient. Thank you. I need to think for a while and get some sleep."

"Shall we come back tomorrow?" Denise asks.

Aliyah dries her eyes before looking at us. "Please. Both of you are welcome. I just…" She gasps in a breath with a grimace and sighs it out. "I am a mess. I hope to be in better shape tomorrow after the surgery."

Denise gets off my lap and leans over to gently kiss Aliyah's forehead. "Sweet dreams, Aliyah."

I follow and squeeze her shoulder gently rather than kissing her. I can't imagine she would be comfortable with that from me right now. "Goodnight, Aliyah. Good luck with the surgery," I tell her.

Denise takes my hand as we walk down the corridor. I walk her to her rental and kiss her. We end up kissing each other for quite a while before I open her door. "Be safe, Darlin'," I tell her. She smiles at me brightly and drives off as I walk to my truck.

Denise beats me home by enough to have a glass of water for me when I walk in the door.

Denise lays her head on my chest as we hold one another. After a minute she raises her head and looks up at me. "You showered," she says with a smile.

"I had to. We worked out heavily with staves. Aliyah would have gone into cardiac arrest from the smell alone," I quip.

She looks at me with hooded eyes, "I like the smell of your sweat."

"Weirdo."

"Your weirdo," she replies immediately.

"Good thing," I tell her.

Denise says, "Sir, I may have to start wearing panties for yoga class. I was thinking about you after our call, and as I was doing Downward

Dog and pressing back, feeling the pull in my muscles. Then I thought about you walking up, ripping my tights open, and sliding your fat cock into my dripping pussy. My tights were sodden in no time. I was quite embarrassed."

She has a glint in her eye. I smile and tell her, "Show me."

I WAKE UP TO A MOIST SENSATION BELOW MY WAISTLINE AS MY BODY is rapidly approaching a climax.

I look down into Denise's eyes as she bobs up and down on my cock, "Guh-good morning...shit! I'm gonna come!" Denise moves frantically and her eyes sparkle with glee as I lose it and start shooting my jism into her eager mouth.

I return to reality as Denise crawls up my body to lay on top of me. She is still wearing her poet's shirt. "Good morning, Guru," she says.

"Guru?"

She nods, "That's the 'official' name for a yoga teacher. You taught me a lot last night, Guru."

I laugh out loud. "You're incorrigible, Pet."

"Thank you, Sir." She presses her breasts into my chest and kisses me.

After releasing my mouth she says, "I'm ready to make this legal whenever you are, Marc." Her smile is brilliant.

I nod. "I suppose I should call your father and ask for your hand."

She gives me a raspberry, and I cock an eyebrow in return. She says, "My father has refused to talk to me since I married Daniel. Mom and I email, but Dad acts like he disowned me."

"Oh!" My mind is blown over how a parent could do that. "Well, I need to get you a ring, propose properly, after that I'm fine with going to a Justice of the Peace."

"I wonder if Chief Justice Morrison would marry us," she ponders. "Maybe we could have Liyana design our rings. She's not terribly expensive, and she does nice work."

I nod. "I'm fine with that. I think my Dad would like to be there."

Denise nods, "I'll ask Aliyah if she'll be my Maid of Honor again."

"Are you sure?" I ask.

Denise nods vigorously. "Yesterday, she placed her hand on both of ours. I know her well enough to know that was a deliberate choice. I don't think she will want to pursue a romantic relationship despite the looks and the 'marrying someone else' comment. If she tells me she does, then I'm going to follow the sage advice of Sir."

I chuckle, "I think that's the first time anyone has insinuated that I have wisdom."

"Give yourself some credit, Marc," she tells me. She sits up and strips her poet's shirt off her body.

I sit up and hold her naked body close as my hands roam her delicious flesh and my lips reconnect with hers.

Denise stands on the bed and jumps off the mattress, holding her breasts as she lands. She says, "It's time to get ready for work. I need a shower since someone dragged me to bed dirty last night."

I roll out of bed and shut off my alarm. "I'll get breakfast going. How's chocolate oatmeal sound?"

"Wonderful. Or we could have ice cream for breakfast. It made a great dinner last night after you wore me out," she says as she turns on the shower.

I fondle her body as she holds a hand under the spray. "We will not be making a habit of that, Pet."

She turns to kiss me once the water temperature meets her satisfaction and steps into the shower.

I pee and wash up before pulling on some sweats and slippers. I grab my pistol out of the nightstand and head to the kitchen.

Later, Denise appears in a navy knit dress with gold buttons from throat to hemline. We share a breakfast of oatmeal and toast with butter and Boursin cheese. She tells me about Aliyah's surgery today. The idea is to repair her cheekbone and any gross muscle damage. They think her left lower eyelid will always sag, but they won't know until her face heals and has time to strengthen the facial muscles.

Denise says Aliyah is not enthusiastic about the thought of going through multiple surgeries, especially for cosmetic purposes, so she's hopeful her face will eventually heal.

I tell Denise about the class with Karen on Saturday and Sunday morning. She plans to ride along and practice at the range before we both go to visit Aliyah.

We clean up the kitchen, and I get Denise safely on the road. I brush my teeth, get dressed, and go see Dad.

Dad's having a bad day. He finishes breakfast shortly after I sit down and pronounces, "I want to go to bed."

I wave Kelly over, and she calls Gretchen to help. Gretchen meets me at the door of the common room as I wheel Dad back to his room. Gretchen and I help him get to the bathroom, which he manages to use without making a big mess. Afterward, we help him into bed. I kiss his forehead, and Gretchen and I leave him to sleep. I think he's unconscious before I pass through the door.

Gretchen rubs my shoulder and says, "He's okay, Marcus. He's been doing very well for several days. He said he didn't sleep well last night. The night nurse heard him yelling in his sleep several times during the night. She sat with him for a while and held his hand."

I sigh and look at the ground. "Yeah, Vietnam comes back to visit him. I remember Mom talking about him waking up in the middle of the night yelling."

Suddenly there is a very warm, firm Gretchen hugging me. She says, "We'll take care of him."

I embrace her briefly and reply, "I know. You guys are the best." Despite some of the stuff she has to deal with here, she smells great. I back away from her hug awkwardly. "Well, have a great day, Gretchen."

I drive home and get back to work on the Buffalo Soldiers. I finish it up around 12:30, so I have a light lunch and start looking at the two editing jobs I picked up yesterday. One is a short novel with a fixed price agreement that equates to about five hours of work. The other is a history textbook, which is an hourly job from a small publishing house.

I spend about two hours on the novel before taking a break to do a tire workout and some karate forms. About five o'clock I go inside for a shower. Denise sends me a text that she's going to see Aliyah at six and she expects to be home around eight-to-eight-thirty.

I make a grocery list, and drive into Carbondale to the store. I should have done this on the way back from the nursing home. This is the only grocer for a couple of country communities. As a result, the little store is quite busy as people stop in on the way home.

I find almost everything on my list. The butcher says they can have chorizo for me early tomorrow morning, so we agreed that I would be there around 10:00.

Upon returning home, I put some beans on to soak before making myself a dinner of roasted broccoli and cauliflower, roasted chicken, and sourdough bread with butter and Havarti cheese. I put some meat and vegetables in a casserole to keep it warm for Denise.

I got two texts as I was eating. One was from the real estate agent saying everything recorded and funded. I now own the farm. The other text is from Martin Greenbaum saying he can install the safe in my truck tomorrow. I agree to be there at 11:00.

I work some more until Denise gets home. She arrives a little before nine o'clock. I serve her some roasted vegetables and chicken with a glass of wine.

"Thank you, Marc," she says tiredly.

"You are welcome, Love. How did it go with Aliyah?" I ask.

"The surgery went well," she says. "The doctor is confident that the cheekbone and the major muscles will fully recover. He's much more pessimistic about the muscles on the lower lid of the eye. He expects the lid will always droop. He doesn't think a cosmetic surgeon can do much. Muhaimin, Aliyah's father, told her that he has a friend in London that does all of the work on celebrities in the UK. He might be able to help, but we need to let her heal for a couple of years first. Muhaimin also has an acquaintance in Kansas City that does a lot of eye cosmetic surgery work. He's arranging for a second opinion."

Denise takes a sip of wine. "I also got a call from my insurance. My Inifinti is totaled. I need to buy a new car."

"When will the insurance money settle?" I ask.

"Within two weeks," she says. "It could be worse."

"Maybe we make Saturday a day in town," I offer. "Go to the range, visit Aliyah, buy a car. Or Sunday could work."

"I think I'll just buy one off Carvana or Vroom," she says with a sigh. "I always hate car shopping. I feel like an antelope surrounded by lions. Plus, they all talk to my breasts."

I chuckle, "I'm sorry, Pet. Shall we sit on the couch and cuddle while you shop?"

"Okay, but is it too early to say I would like to have sex before we fall asleep?" she asks with a smile.

"Not too early at all, Pet."

8

TIME FLIES

The rest of the week passed rapidly. Friday I visited with Dad, picked up my groceries, and went to Martin's place in Scranton. He introduced me to two dogs he had in a kennel when I arrived - a five-year-old brindle Bull Mastiff named Remus and a two-year-old Rottweiler named Buster. The Rottweiler grew up with the Mastiff, so the owner wanted to keep them together. I sat in the kennel with them while Martin installed the safe. Then he had me snap leashes on them and lead them around. When I opened the door to the pickup to send PayPal to the breeder, both dogs jumped in.

The dogs loved Denise. She was a little shy with them at first because of their size, but they are both very loving and intelligent dogs. They figured out quickly that she is the alpha female to my alpha male, and we all got along great. We put big dog beds by the fireplace in the living room and the world's largest dog door between the kitchen and the garage - so much for 'animals live outside.' I was worried about critters getting in through the dog door, but it had a tight enough spring with a good seal all around the opening. Apparently it wasn't going to be a problem. The dogs could push it open, but they had to work at it. I didn't feel cold air coming through on particularly cold nights, so we counted it as good enough. I put a less expensive version in the north entry door to the garage.

I took the CCW course that weekend and spent some time practicing at the range with Denise. Saturday we had pizza for a late lunch and visited Aliyah for nearly three hours. She had difficulty talking due to the post-op swelling, but she said it's already much better than yesterday. She held onto Denise's hand for most of the visit as we shared the story of how we met and our adventures with Clan Connolly. When I told her about what Joe Hesse said, she decided that she is going to write another story about them. I told her to give me some warning, so I could be prepared to protect her. She looked at me warily but eventually relented.

I called ahead and told the home that Denise and I would eat dinner with Dad. He woke up from his nap about thirty minutes before we arrived, and we had a great time visiting with all the folks at the home. Denise excused herself to use the restroom after dinner. She was gone long enough that I began to worry, but she walked in arm-in-arm with Gretchen just as I was about ready to go find her. Their heads were leaning towards each other conspiratorially, the taller blond practically leaning on Denise. Gretchen put Dad to bed after that, and I forgot all about it until much later.

Sunday was pretty much a repeat of Saturday other than Denise and I met with Liyana Sadduzai to design wedding rings in the hospital waiting room.

Aliyah went home Monday to begin her recovery. Aliyah had a consultation with the cosmetic surgeon in Kansas City thanks to Muhaimin's referral. The surgeon recommended stitching the lower lid to get it back into position to protect the eye sooner rather than later and to prevent muscle atrophy. Aliyah accepted that she would have a one-inch scar, but she preferred that to a drooping lower lid. I drove Liyana and Aliyah to Kansas City for the procedure and brought them back the same day.

Denise and Liyana took turns staying with Aliyah overnight for the two-week convalescence. Denise confided in me that she and Aliya spent a lot of time holding each other, talking, kissing, and caressing.

Apparently, there was one occasion where pussies were ground rather vigorously into thighs, but that's as far as things went. Denise said Aliyah acted like nothing happened the next morning every time.

The newspaper let Aliyah work from home for a couple of weeks after the cast came off her hand, but within a few days after her eye surgery, she started going into the office for a daily meeting with her editor. I met with her at the library in Topeka a couple of times to talk about my run-ins with the Connolly family and what Joe Hesse said. I arranged to drive her down to the nursing home one Wednesday afternoon to interview Joe.

I had a steady flow of editing work, including a second pass on the Buffalo Soldiers book. I also wrote three different articles that got picked up by Reader's Digest, Better Homes and Gardens, and Mother Earth News respectively.

Martin Greenbaum called to say that he had a couple more dogs. I went over to see them. They were Bull Mastiff - Great Dane hybrids with brindle pelts. The breeder called them 'Cuon' after the hounds in one of his favorite fantasy book series. I'm not sure if they are what the author imagined, but they are impressive. We get along well, and they respond to my commands well. So Harry and Muffy joined the family.

Liyana created a beautiful set of matching gold bands inscribed with ivy vines and leaves. Denise's is a matching pair of engraved, three-millimeter gold bands - one with a half-carat faceted diamond mounted on it, whereas mine has a small diamond embedded in an eight-millimeter band.

Liyana Sadduzai invited Denise and me to celebrate *Eid Milad un Nabi*, the prophet Muhammad's birthday, with their family. I proposed to Denise the following weekend at Chez Yasu. Aliyah and her parents witnessed. Denise introduced me to Chief Justice Constance, 'call me Connie,' Morrison. She agreed to officiate the wedding.

Aliyah stayed with us on the second weekend in November. She was enchanted with the farm as much as Denise was. She was a little wary of all the dogs, but they won her over after we all took a long walk in the pasture. Aliyah was also a little put off with us carrying weapons, but she proclaimed she understood why we would. She wasn't interested in trying to fire them. We all cooked meals together, visited, walked the farm repeatedly, and sat in the living room chatting in the evenings. Frequently, Aliyah sat between Denise and me on the couch. There was a lot of flirtatious touching between the ladies, and Aliyah made a point to hug me every night before she went to bed.

Denise and I kept our lovemaking pretty quiet during Aliyah's visit, but we made up for it by tying Denise to the bed after Aliyah went home. The dogs got pretty curious about Denise's moans, groans, and screams, but they had heard us often enough by that point that they just stuck their noses in the bedroom to ensure we were both okay before they returned to the living room.

Aliyah's wounds were healing nicely. Denise said Aliyah was obsessing about how bright the scar below her eye was, but she counted herself lucky the injury didn't impinge on her vision.

I thought things were going well. I should have known better.

It's the Friday before Thanksgiving. Denise's phone wakes us up a little after five in the morning. She answers, "Hellooo?" ... "Aliyah?"... "Honey, slow down. What happened?"... "We're coming for you. We'll be there in less than an hour. Can you hold on until then?"... "Great, just ask them to stay there until we get there. Are your parents okay?"... "Good."... "Honey, I love you, too. See you soon."

Denise disconnects the phone and gets out of bed. "Someone showed up at Aliyah's door about an hour ago. She was staying with her parents for the night, but the Ring doorbell at her condo woke her up. The guy told her to drop the charges against the Connollys and threatened Aliyah and her family."

"Oh shit!" I exclaim as I turn on the light and get out of bed to pull on clothes. "Is she at her house now or still at her parents?" I pull on jeans, hiking boots, a tech fabric t-shirt and a light sweater.

She says, "Her parents' house. The police went to her condo, but the guy was long gone. The Ring video caught him as he walked up. He covered the lens, but there's plenty of footage to identify him. He spoke into the device, so everything is recorded." Denise pulls on panties, cargo pants, a sports bra and a tech fabric sweater. She pulls her hair back into a tail and puts on a ball cap that velcros around her ponytail. I pull out the Armscor VR80, the Glock, Denise's Walther, and her Benelli. We load them all, and ensure we've got two spare magazines for each pistol and the Armscor. I pull the Shockwave from under the bed and clear it before loading it with 3" double-aught buckshot. I put the Glock in a quick-draw holster I picked up when I took the CCW class. It's strapped to my thigh, I have my clip knife in my pocket, and I pull on the shoulder rig for the M&P. A light windbreaker goes over that.

On a whim, Denise grabs the Ruger pistols, a spare magazine each, and loads them both. We load everything into her new all-wheel drive QX60. The Rugers go in the safe under the driver seat. The VR80 goes on the floor behind Denise where I can reach it. The Shockwave is on the floor under Denise's feet. I drive her SUV out of the garage, happy that we've started combat parking as a common practice.

Twenty-five minutes later, we are pulling into the Sadduzai house, a large brick house on the south bank of the Kansas River. There are three police cars in the circle drive. Denise calls Liyana, and an empty garage bay opens. I back the SUV into it and kill the lights.

We lock the vehicle and follow Liyana inside. Aliyah is sitting on the sofa looking shell-shocked.

Denise calls out, "Aliyah!"

Aliyah looks up, launches toward Denise, and wraps her in a tight hug, sobbing into my fiancé's neck. I cuddle up to her and wrap them both tightly in my arms. Aliyah releases an arm and snakes it around my neck as she sobs on Denise's shoulder. We hold her until her sobs quiet. I offer her my handkerchief to dry her eyes. She gives me a look of gratitude as she wipes her face.

We get her seated between Denise and Liyana as a couple of detectives in suits are escorted in by one of the officers.

Aliyah pulls out her phone and shows Denise the video footage.

Denise growls, "It's fucking Michael Connolly." I've never seen her so angry.

The officer asks, "That's the name of the guy in the video?"

"Yes," Denise fumes. She leans forward to look at Aliyah's mother. "I'm sorry, Liyana. You deserve better behavior from me."

Liyana notes Denise's hand on Aliyah's knee. She pats Denise's hand and says, "You are forgiven, Denise. I agree with the sentiment, even if it is uncharitable."

Denise looks at the officer. "His name is Michael Seamus Connolly. His family calls him Mick. The last I heard of him was that he is a police officer in Hays. The last time I saw him was at my wedding over five years ago, but the video shows he hasn't changed much - a little heavier perhaps. His brothers were mortally afraid of his temper. His father, Seamus Connolly, is the police chief in Salina and was arrested recently for attacking Marcus, my fiancé." She points at me.

The officer turns to look at me, and I wave. He takes in the holster strapped to my leg and scowls at me. "Michael's younger brothers beat Aliyah just short of killing her. After that, they tried to kill both Denise and me by ramming her car before trying to beat me with a sledgehammer. Then the elder one..."

"Sean," Denise interjects.

"...Sean tried to sneak into the hospital to finish off Aliyah, killing an orderly and attacking two policeman in the process. Then Seamus assaulted me. I'm not taking any chances with this family."

Denise says, "There are several cousins in law enforcement in Abilene, Salina, Hays, and Russell. If I remember correctly there may be one in Manhattan or Junction City, too."

One of the suits says, "I'm agent Howell, KBI. Chief Connolly made bail after arraignment. We have been pressuring the Salina mayor to put him on suspension, but the guy is seriously afraid of repercussions. I was hoping they would stay quiet until the new mayor comes on board in January." He sighs. "We don't have the resources to deal with this. Since this involves more and more law enforcement and has the appearance of organized crime, we called in the FBI. This is Special Agent Johnson."

Johnson says, "The SAC from Kansas City has taken a task force of KBI, state troopers, and our agents to Salina. I would like to interview everyone here again."

Liyana says, "I will put coffee and tea on. Excuse me." She gets up and hurries to the kitchen. Muhaimin takes her seat.

Agent Johnson and Agent Howell take me to an adjacent TV room and grill me. I repeat everything I recall about each incident with the Connolly family from Daniel's attack through Seamus' attack at the Supreme Court building. I also share what I recall of Joe Hesse's story. When I'm done, Liyana hands me a cup of coffee. I give her a hug and take my coffee outside.

I lean against one of the pillars and listen absentmindedly to the chatter of the officers stationed on the porch. I look out over the manicured yard and watch a car go by - one of the newer Lincolns. I can't help but laugh when I compare it to the beige Chevy parked at the curb on the street.

It takes me a moment to figure out that there are no other cars parked on the street in this neighborhood. I walk inside and beckon for one of the officers to follow me.

I ask, "Did you notice the beige Chevy parked on the street?"

"What?" he asked perplexed.

"I only recall seeing one car parked on the street in this neighborhood - that Chevy. It's right at the bottom of the Sadduzai yard. I see a lot of Lincolns, Cadillacs, Lexus, and Infinitis driving by - no Chevys."

The officer looks into the room, "Sarge! A minute please."

The sergeant joins us. The officer explains, "We may have someone watching the house. There's a beige Chevy on the curb."

"Did we have officers come here directly from Miss Sadduzai's condo?" the sergeant asks.

The officer says, "I think Thompson and Morgan did."

I say, "They're cops. They may be listening to your radio, too."

The sergeant gives me the stink eye. He looks over his shoulder, "Thompson. C'mere."

The officer that questioned me about carrying a weapon came over. The sergeant says, "I want you and Shea to grab your partners and mount up. There's a beige Chevy at the bottom of the hill. You drive past them and block them to the rear. Radio silence. Shea, you put your front bumper right in front of the Chevy - and I mean inches in front of it. Apprehend whoever it is, search their vehicles for weapons, and take the occupants to the station for questioning. Clear?"

"Yes, Sergeant," they respond in unison like good soldiers.

The Sergeant says, "Brown. Take over for Mason and Morgan on the front door."

Another officer responds, "Yes, Sergeant."

The officers all file out, and the sergeant talks quietly to the agents as they escort Aliyah back into the living room. They nod to the sergeant's comments and escort Denise to the TV room.

Ten minutes later, the sergeant approaches me. "Two off-duty cops. One from Manhattan named Connolly. One from Abilene named Morrisey. Good eye, Mr. Hough."

I tell him, "Thanks, Sergeant." We shake hands, and then I walk over to sit beside Aliyah.

Aliyah crawls onto my lap. No one else is nearby, so I murmur quietly to the distraught woman. "Probably not as comfortable as Denise's lap."

Aliyah hiccups a short laugh. She murmurs into my chest, "Hers is nearly as firm. Yours is likely to raise fewer questions from my parents."

I chuckle, "For certain." I caress her arm gently as my other hand winds behind her back to rest on her thigh. "Denise and I will take care of you, Aliyah. You come stay with us. I'll drive you both into work and bring you home each day until we put all this nonsense to bed."

She nearly growls. "This fear is why I wrote the story in the first place. These people have been running amok for decades - ruining people's lives. I ran across the story at Denise's wedding; the brothers were boasting about some of the crimes they committed. I just didn't overhear enough to write a story then."

"How's the new story coming?" I ask.

"It's going to be a week-long series. There's too much material for one edition," she says. "Your story may be the focus of one edition."

"I don't need the publicity, Aliyah," I tell her sternly. I pause before asking, "Honey, will you let me teach you how to shoot?"

She whines slightly. "Marc, I don't want to be that kind of person. I believe in the rule of law. Societal boundaries let us all flourish. This cowboy behavior has to stop."

"I agree with your sentiment," I tell her. "However, I have to face the reality that we are being hunted by people that do not believe the same. You and Denise are too important to me. I will fight to protect you both."

Aliyah sits up to look me in the eye. After a moment she caresses my cheek and kisses the other one. "No wonder Denise loves you so much." She lays her head back on my shoulder, the silk of her Hijab tickling my neck.

"I'm very lucky, Aliyah. I was adrift until we found each other," I confess as I caress her arm.

After sitting quietly for a minute, she says, "Maybe. When we are on the farm I will try shooting."

I tell her, "I picked up a small crossbow and a taser. We could start with those if you like."

"We'll see," she replies with a sad smile.

Liyana walks in with a cart of coffee service - a closed carafe, sugar, milk, and fresh cups. She looks at me holding her daughter with a questioning look. Aliyah slides off my lap and walks off with a gentle caress of her mother's shoulder.

I stand and pick up my empty mug from the coaster, and Liyana fills my coffee.

"What is happening with my daughter, Marcus?" she asks.

"Her sense of social justice has put her in the crosshairs of some very bad men," I respond.

Liyana's eyes look deep into my soul. She steps closer and murmurs, "My Aliyah does not let men touch her. She had a bad experience when she was younger. She struggles with hugs from her father and brothers. The dates we arranged for her to meet eligible men always resulted in comments about how cold she is."

"She's not cold. I think she's a very warm person despite having reasons to be very guarded," I murmur back in equally quiet tones.

"She sat on your lap, Marcus. She let you hold her," LIyana says. "She does not do that. I thought she might be looking to Denise for a life partner, but you have taken Denise off the market. So of course, my daughter would decide you are the one man she can let touch her."

"Denise loves her, Liyana. She's never had a better friend than Aliyah," I try as an explanation.

Fortunately, Denise rescues me. She just lays it out there. "Liyana, if Marcus had not come into my life, I might have turned to Aliyah like you are thinking. It's not something I've done before, but I love her regardless. It might have worked." Denise cuddles up close to me. "But I have found Marcus. I'm trying desperately to ensure Aliyah knows that I still love her." She looks up to me as she says, "I think it's safe to say that Marcus is growing to love her, too. We're both growing to love your family and think of you as our own."

Liyana cocks an eyebrow at us and says quietly. "Our faith provides different options than what local laws might accept. There are ways," she finishes cryptically. She kisses each of us on the cheek and walks back to the kitchen with a mysterious smile.

I wrap Denise up tightly in a hug, and we surrender to the warmth of our shared embrace.

Denise murmurs into my ear, "I'm not certain what to think about Liyana's comments. Interesting, don't you think?"

"Definitely," I agree. "Almost as interesting as the fact that Aliyah crawled up on my lap so I would hold her."

"Really?" Denise is surprised. "She was sexually assaulted in middle school. She doesn't like men touching her."

"That's what Liyana said. Aliyah called me 'Marc,' too. Where did she learn that?" I ask with a grin.

"Noooo," Denise says. The smirk on her face tells me it's not a surprise to her.

At that point, Aliyah rejoins us with a gym bag over her shoulder. She's in the same grey sweatpants, grey crewneck sweatshirt, and white silk hijab as before, but with the addition of trainers and a long, patchwork quilted coat that reaches to her knees.

Aliyah says quietly, "The agents said I can leave. I need to pick up some clothes at my place, and then we can leave town. Let me say goodbye to my parents."

I drain my coffee, and Denise and I follow Aliyah to the kitchen.

As Aliyah hugs her father awkwardly, Denise and I hug her mother. "Liyana, thank you for keeping me caffeinated," I tell her.

Liyana hugs us both closely and kisses our cheeks. "Keep my daughter safe," she says sternly.

"We will," Denise says a moment before I do.

Muhaimin shakes our hands. "Take care of my little girl, you two."

"We will," I say, beating Denise by half a second.

We leave the kitchen for the garage. I detour to talk to the Sergeant. "We're going to run by her condo to pick up some clothes, and then we're all leaving town. Are you going to keep surveillance here?"

He nods. "Her condo, too.

I ask, "Do you think we could get a car to run interference as we leave town? I'm thinking about blocking the highway just past Forbes field for about five minutes."

The sergeant says, "Normally I'd dismiss that without a second thought, but given the shit you folks have been through, I'll call the Shawnee County Sheriff to see if they'll play along. It's outside our jurisdiction."

"Thanks, Sergeant," I tell him.

The ladies are waiting on me, so I rejoin them. Aliyah leads us into the garage. Denise rides shotgun, and Aliyah sits behind her with her gym bag on the seat behind me.

Aliyah's condo is off Burlingame Road. There is a police car parked in front of Aliyah's condo when we pull up. I tell her, "Wait until I come to get you, Aliyah."

"Okay, Marc," she answers.

I smile at Denise and tell her, "Keep watch, Love. Mostly to the front, but check to the rear regularly, too. The police are going to be watching us, so you can't assume they are watching your back. Keys are in the column."

"Got it," my fiancé says with a serious expression. I give her a quick kiss and get out of the SUV.

I hold my hands out to my side, and a policeman gets out of the car. The other one stays in the driver's seat. They're both looking at the pistol strapped to my leg.

I call out, "Hello, officer. I have Ms. Sadduzai in the truck. She would like to get some clothes and personal belongings before we leave town. I will pull my wallet out of my left front pocket if you would like."

He nods, "Yeah, let's see it."

I pull out my money clip, extract my license, and hand it over to the officer. He reminds me of the actor Kevin Hart but taller. The officer looks at my license and hands it back to me before saying, "Sergeant Reynolds told me you were coming."

I ask, "Is anyone watching the back?"

"Not constantly. We take patrols around the back at irregular intervals. If she was staying, we'd have patrols both front and back for a while," he says.

"Yeah, too much demand for too few officers. Can't keep 'em there indefinitely. I guess we need to put this to bed quickly," I say to demonstrate my understanding.

"You sound like you know," he says.

"Not really," I answer. "I was an MP in Afghanistan - National Guard. There are similarities, but I know it's not the same as what you go through."

He nods and says, "Let us clear the house first."

I nod my agreement, "Go heavy. These guys have shown an indecent willingness to use violence."

He nods, "Roger." He waves at his partner and points at the shotgun. The driver grabs the weapon and gets out of the car. He's a short Hispanic guy that stands about 5'5" and has shoulders that look nearly as broad as he is tall. Both officers don helmets, and I go to get the keys from Aliyah.

I have Aliyah put the Shockwave in her gym bag and hand me the VR80. Denise grabs the Benelli and the car keys.

Aliyah follows me as I watch the streets. I hang the shotgun from its sling pointed at the ground and hand the keys to 'Officer Hart.' Denise is close behind with her shotgun at port arms.

The driver asks, "Is that a Benelli M4? What mods do you have on it?"

"It's stock," Denise says. "I've been shooting shotguns since I was fourteen, so I figured stock was good enough. The semi-auto reduces the recoil pretty nicely. I only wish I had a magazine like Marcus' weapon. Reloading under pressure with a tube magazine is a bitch. I'd almost rather deal with a break action for quick reloads."

The guy is definitely in love. Eventually, he picks his jaw off the ground and looks at mine. "Armscor VR80, semi-auto from Rock Island Armory. Why didn't you get the 9-round mag?" he asks.

"They didn't have it in stock. I have some on order," I tell him.

"We've got this old Mossberg 500," he says.

"I like Mossbergs. I've got their Shockwave. Handy little weapon," I tell.

"Enough stroking your gun, Roderick. Let's move," his partner says.

'Officer Hart' unlocks the door, and they disappear inside the house. They return shortly. 'Hart' says, "It seems clear, we checked closets, behind shower curtains, and under the beds. The patio door was locked. You should be good. We'll guard the door."

I lead the way into the house. We escort Aliyah to the garage to retrieve a large suitcase and a small roll-aboard. I carry those upstairs to her master suite and leave the ladies to pack. I go downstairs to her office and grab her computer, its power supply, and a phone charger from her desk. Her normal messenger bag is sitting on the floor beside her desk, so I set all of them on a corner of her immaculate desk.

About fifteen minutes later the ladies come down carrying the roll-aboard. I explain what I've done so far. Aliyah kisses my cheek, and I head upstairs to grab her suitcase off her bed. I also grab her pillow - it's the one thing that can make sleeping in a strange place better.

Denise hands me the keys, and I lug the heavy bag to the SUV. I put Aliyah's pillow in the back seat. Denise leads Aliyah out of the house. Denise is holding her weapon at the ready with Aliyah's messenger bag over her shoulder.

Aliyah drags her other bag, gym bag, and a cooler. As she hands me the cooler, I look at her funny. She says, "I had some perishables in the fridge. I can think of no good reason to waste them."

"Sounds reasonable," I say as I stow the cooler and then the two bags in the back. I call out to the officers, "We're done."

They lock up the house and bring the keys to us. Another car pulls up, and Sergeant Reynolds gets out. He says, "I'm your escort to Forbes. A sheriff's deputy will join us south of the turnpike. Two state troopers will block off the road at Gary Ormsby drive for five minutes after you pass. Another will follow you down to the ramp onto US-75 before he hops on the highway and continues south on his patrol. At that point, you're on your own."

"Got it," I tell him. "Thanks for the support."

9

GOING HOME

The ladies are seated and buckled in. I hand Aliyah the VR80 and retrieve the Shockwave from the gym bag. I get in, hand the weapon to Denise, and pull away from the curb.

I make my way to I-470 and drive east, exiting onto Topeka Boulevard. Events transpire as Sergeant Reynolds explained them. The deputy pulls out of the old western wear store next to where the Dairy Queen used to be. Four highway patrol units are parked at Gary Orsmby, and pull out after our car and my two trail cars pass. I see two units turn on the flashing lights to slow traffic, one runs ahead and blocks the right curb to the centerline, and a fourth one falls in behind my convoy. The two with lights on pull into the gap to block traffic. Sergeant Reynolds and the deputy pull off at the entrance for Heartland Motorway, and the one trooper stays about three car lengths back.

I get on the spur of the 'new' US-75 and the state trooper falls farther back and continues to follow. I pass a parked car just before the Wakarusa River. The car pulls out after we pass. It follows us for about a mile before the trooper pulls him over. I continue south to the Scranton-Overbrook exit, turn east, and head back north on Adams Road. Five miles later, we're pulling into the driveway.

Remus, Buster, Harry, and Muffy meet us in the driveway. I back the SUV into the garage. Denise unlocks the house and returns to take the weapons inside. Harry and Muffy slide past Denise to lay on the dog beds by the fireplace while Aliyah and I grab bags and carry them inside. Remus and Buster stayed outside. It's almost like the dogs have set a rota for who has inside security and outside security.

I put Aliyah's bags in the room she used before - my old bedroom. It's a little small. I'll have to spend some time either getting the upstairs set up as a bedroom or moving my office up there, so I can give Aliyah my office. We can figure that out over time.

As we did during Aliyah's visit, we all congregate in the kitchen and dining room. I pour water for everyone, and Denise brings out cleaning kits for the weapons. We sit around the table and clear each weapon, wipe each down, oil the moving parts, and run a very lightly oiled swab down each barrel. After the light cleaning, we function-check and load them, leaving the breach empty. We explain what we were doing to Aliyah. When we are done, I set the Shockwave on top of the refrigerator, I keep my Glock on my hip, and my M&P goes into the nightstand. Denise keeps her Walther clipped on the back of her cargo pants. The rest all go back into the gun safe.

I can tell Aliyah is uncomfortable with all the weapons around. I pull her out of her chair and hug her. "They are tools, Aliyah. They are not toys or a hobby or some misguided expression of exercising our rights. They are tools to protect our lives and property."

She nods shyly and hugs me back. I kiss her forehead and drag her to the kitchen. We make a big brunch of omelettes, sautéed spinach, freshly baked rolls from the freezer, cold cuts, orange juice, coffee, and tea. We all loosen up as we work together to prepare the meal.

I call the nursing home to tell them we will be down to visit Dad around four-thirty to join him for dinner. They're having pork chops, so I order the alternate meal for Aliyah - fish sticks and fries. She smiles at the thought of it.

I grab the small crossbow and a handful of bolts from my office, and take the ladies out to the machine shed. When I open the big barn doors, I discover an opossum curled up under the workbench. Buster growls at it, but it doesn't move. I grab a long-handled shovel and carry it outside. Denise follows me with the Shockwave.

Aliyah asks, "Are you going to kill it?"

"Nah," I answer. "Not unless it attacks. I don't see any remnants of foam around its mouth, so it's likely not rabid - just looking for a safe place to sleep. I'm pretty certain they are nocturnal." I set down the shovel and slide the animal off it behind Denise's POD. I back away and add, "It's breathing got faster after I picked it up, but it just laid there limp. That's why they call feigning sleep 'playing possum.' It's a defense mechanism for the opossum."

"Oh," Aliyah says a moment before Denise does.

I smirk and lead the ladies back into the shed, and I point at a four-by-four sheet of one-inch plywood hanging about two feet off the ground. It has a painted human silhouette with a bullseye painted center-of-mass.

I tell Aliyah, "This is the practice target. Note the human silhouette. It's meant to emphasize that humans are our biggest threat and helps build the mindset that we may have to kill one or more to survive."

Her eyes are like saucers. She gulps and nods. Denise starts to comfort her but stops herself short. I can see from her expression that she understands that Aliyah needs to learn this.

I pick up the crossbow from the bench. "This is a pistol-sized crossbow. It's not made for long-range shooting. I would say the maximum effective range is twenty feet, and I recommend saving your shot until they are within ten feet if you can." I walk down to the target and pick up a two-inch thick phonebook on a string. I hang it in front of the bullseye and return to a line on the floor ten feet from the target. Denise gives Aliyah a gentle push towards me, and she tentatively steps up next to me.

I hold the weapon out to her and demonstrate how to cock it. "To make it ready to fire, you have to cock it, like an old firearm. Press down on this little red button and pull the nose down like this." I demonstrate.

I put a bolt, or small arrow, in the weapon, and grasp it by the front and back pistol grips before firing it. I have gotten damned accurate with the thing. Denise is better with guns than I am, but I'm freaking deadly with a crossbow. It's like a Zen exercise for me. I hit the center of the small bullseye painted on the phone book. It's helping my marksmanship with firearms, too.

I hand it to Aliyah. "Cock it, Aliyah." She looks it over for a moment and then presses the correct button. She struggles but does get it cocked.

"Good job, Sweetie." I take it back, load a bolt, and aim to the immediate right of the first bolt. It hits my aim point with a thunk. I hand it back to her. "Try to quickly snap it rather than muscling it."

Aliyah has an easier time of it this time. She hands it back to me, and I load it. I murmur, "Upper left corner" before I fire the bolt into the small hole the string runs through that holds it in place."

"Let's go look at these for a moment," I say as I offer Aliyah the crook of my left arm. She loops her arm through mine, and we walk up to the target. I pull off the string that is suspending the phonebook in front of the target, and then I pry the phonebook off the plywood.

I show the points of the bolts sticking through the back of the thick book. Aliyah gives me a surprised look. "I did not think that such a small weapon could be that strong."

I nod my understanding. "Part of it is the distance from the target. Part of it is the Topeka phone book isn't that thick. I fired from ten feet. At twelve feet, the points won't stick out the back but will penetrate most of the way through. At twenty feet, you better hit a soft, vital target like the eyes, throat, solar plexus, or femoral artery. Even then, heavy clothing could defeat the penetrating power. The point of this exercise isn't to give you a lethal weapon, but to give you a tool to practice marksmanship without the noise of a firearm to let build the attitude of readiness to defend yourself."

She says, "I don't think I could ever shoot anyone."

I reach out and grab her by the throat and press her against the target. I can see the fear in her eyes. "Imagine I'm Sean Connolly, Aliyah. Any moment leading up to an attack and any moment after an attacker strikes is the time when you have to choose to live. You have to do whatever you can to survive - to stop him from hurting you."

Tears run down Aliyah's face as she gasps, "I can't."

"You can," I tell her. I release her and pull her gently to the side. "Denise come here."

Denise walks up, and I grab her by the throat like I did Aliyah and push her into the target. I wink at Denise, and she starts making choking sounds. I've squeezed her throat more firmly in the bedroom, but Alilyah thinks I'm choking her hard. She looks from Denise to me and back again before she launches at me, hitting my arm and clawing at my face like an angry badger. I release Denise and wrap Aliyah in my arms to stop her attack. Aliyah snatches the crossbow out of my hand and swings it at my head.

I snatch it out of her hand, but not before the bow makes a glancing blow off the top of my head. Denise wraps her arms around Aliyah. She murmurs, "Stop now, Allie. Stop. We're just training."

Aliyah slowly calms down and stares at me. The tears slowly drip from her face. "Why?" she asks. "Why did you do that to me?"

I reach out to cup her face, but she slaps my hand away. "WHY?" she screams. She is seriously angry.

I set the crossbow on the ground and grab both of her slender wrists in one of my hands and cup her face in the other as she struggles.

I answer her quietly but fiercely, "Because we love you, Aliyah. You are nearly as dear to me as you are to Denise. I want you to live! I will try to be there to protect you always, but you are an independent woman. You WILL go off on your own eventually. If something happens when I'm not there to protect you, I want you to live - preferable with little or no injury to yourself."

I remove my hand and pick up the crossbow. "You are precious to us both, Aliyah. I know you are fighting with your stories to make the world a better place, and I admire you for it. But, words won't protect you when they come for you. You have to FIGHT! My love for you means I have to teach you to survive."

Denise kisses her cheek. "Me too, Allie. I will do everything I can to protect you, and that means teaching you to shoot, having Marc teach you to fight, and having a dog with you whenever possible. I will be firm with you too, Love. You will be angry with me."

Aliyah breaks down into sobs again. She turns and rests her head on Denise's shoulder as Denise hugs her. I walk up behind her and hug them both.

Eventually, Aliyah raises her head and says, "I'm sorry, Marc. I think I understand. I probably won't be a very good student, but please do try to teach me."

I kiss the top of her head gently. "I don't know, Aliyah. The way you attacked me when you thought I was hurting Denise makes me think you can be a fierce fighter. We just have to teach you to care about yourself as much as you care for Denise."

"Good luck," she says with a gentle frown.

Denise cups Aliyah's face and says, "I love you, Allie. Your safety is important to me. If you can't fight for yourself, then fight because I will be hurt if you are hurt."

Aliyah caresses Denise's face and kisses her tenderly before turning and walking back to the ten-foot line. She pastes a determined look on her face. "Show me," she says.

I show her how to hold the weapon and sight it. Then I have her cock the weapon and load it. We walk her through firing all twenty target bolts three times. The target is three concentric rings. Aliyah doesn't have a consistent aim, but the last ten bolts she fires are mostly in line with the bullseye and spread across the second and third rings to the right of the target.

We pick up the bolts, and I coach her to squeeze the trigger rather than pulling it. Denise leans back into my arms for a hug as Aliyah fires ten more bolts, and they all hit in the second ring or the bullseye.

"Still pulling to the right," she observes.

I nod, "Yep, but you hit two bullseyes on your first time out. Impressive, Aliyah." Denise slides out of my embrace and gives Aliyah a lover's kiss.

Aliyah looks at me warily. I walk up to her and look down into her wide-open eyes. I tell her, "If you and I had that level of intimacy, I'd be kissing you too, Aliyah. I'm very proud of you."

She kisses my cheek and smiles at me shyly before retrieving her bolts. I give her an armband for her right arm that holds four bolts. "Ah!" she exclaims in recognition. "That will make it easier to load quickly."

"Yes," Denise says. "This time, I want you to deliberately but quickly fire five bolts - one in your hand and four from your quiver.

Focus on good mechanics as Marc taught you, but move smoothly through firing all five bolts. As soon as you pull the trigger the first time, flow through firing the other four. Focus on flowing through the motions rather than hurrying."

Aliyah picks up a bolt, cocks the weapon, and releases a breath. I start the stopwatch on my phone when she first pulls the trigger. The last bolt flies thirty-two seconds later. Denise and I average twenty-to-twenty-five seconds. "Aliyah that was fantastic!"

She grins at us.

After crossbow practice, we shower. Denise and I make love in the shower, so Aliyah is sitting on the couch reading her tablet when we emerge from the bedroom.

Aliyah says with a sardonic grin, "Your bedroom walls are not particularly soundproof."

I chuckle and look at Denise to catch her blushing. "I guess the shower wasn't enough to drown out your screams."

She crosses her eyes and sticks her tongue out in the most adult manner possible. She releases her expression and says, "If you didn't insist on driving me to screaming orgasms it wouldn't be an issue."

I smirk, "You could always safeword, Pet."

She responds, "Not even if you're killing me, Sir." I get another tongue display before she wraps her arms around me and drives that tongue into my mouth. I squeeze her fine ass, eliciting a moan into my mouth.

Aliyah clears her throat, "Kph!"

I chuckle, "I think Aliyah is asking us to take an intermission."

Aliyah stands and asks, "Will this be okay?" She's wearing jeans, a relatively snug tunic, knee-high boots, and an orange print scarf as a hijab. It's the first time I've ever noticed her figure. Before she pulls on a matching knee-length burnt orange sweater, I notice pert breasts, a narrow waist, and slightly flared hips. I catch a glimpse of a nicely compact round tushy as she twists to run her arm into the sleeve of the sweater.

Denise says, "You look great, Aliyah."

I finally collect myself to say, "Yes, you do, Aliyah. Very nice." Denise gives me a knowing grin.

I ask, "Shall we go?"

✣

WE ARRIVED AT DAD'S ROOM AT THE NURSING HOME AS KEVIN WAS assisting him in the bathroom. We waited in the doorway until they walked out, and Kevin sat him in the wheelchair. Denise and I gave Dad hugs and handshakes for Kevin. We introduced Aliyah to them both.

Dad looked at her for a moment. "Are you Muslim?" he asked in his typically direct manner.

Aliyah smiled and said, "Why yes, I am." She cocked her head slightly and teased him. "Let me guess, my stylish head scarf gave me away."

Dad said, "Oh. Yeah, probably. I think you're the first Muslim I've met. You sound like a Brit."

Aliyah nodded, "Well, that's because I grew up in London until I was eight. My accent has softened significantly, so family in London think I sound like a Yank now." She flashed him a bright smile. Her eyes glowed with humor. "When I visit my family in Pakistan, I come back with a stronger Pakistani accent. My language may well be a mess."

Kevin surreptitiously pointed to Dad's chair, and I nodded in response. I said, "Well, Kevin. Since you have Dad all dressed for the prom, I better drive his chariot to dinner."

Kevin smiled gratefully and pointed back to the bathroom. I nodded as I stepped behind Dad's wheelchair. "Here we go, Dad. Hold onto your knickers."

We sat at Dad's table, which they had extended by grouping two normal tables. That let Dad's normal cronies join us. They did manage to get the fish sticks for Aliyah, and we had an enjoyable meal visiting with Dad and his friends.

I think every one of the residents and most of the staff asked Aliyah if she were Muslim. Gretchen was one of the few that didn't, but Kelly apparently was so overwhelmed that she asked twice. Gretchen gave us all hugs before she left, as her shift was over.

After dinner, I retrieved my guitar from the Infiniti and sat in the common room playing my limited repertoire. Many of the residents sang along to the songs they knew - even Denise and Aliyah joined in on some.

Everyone started heading to their rooms at 7:30. Tommy, another aide, helped Dad get ready for bed after all three of us hugged Dad goodnight.

We returned to the farm and visited for several hours. Aliyah sat in one of the recliners and asked about the weapons, so we discussed them for a while. She committed to trying a .22 pistol tomorrow. We talked through her stories about the Connolly family in Salina. After that topic ran dry, Denise talked about one of the cases before the court.

About two minutes into Denise's story, Aliyah got up from the recliner and squeezed between Denise and I on the sofa. Denise started giggling as Aliyah pushed her farther from me until she was satisfied. Aliyah looked back and forth measuring the distance between us and then lay down with her head in Denise's lap and her feet in mine.

I massaged her feet through the thin socks she was wearing, and she hummed her pleasure. I smiled at Denise, and she grinned in return as she focused on me for the rest of her story.

I looked at Aliyah. It appeared she was asleep. I looked at Denise and nodded towards the bedroom. She nodded her agreement. I slid out from under Aliyah's feet, scooped her up into a bridal carry, and carried her to the small bedroom. Denise moved Aliyah's suitcases off the bed, and I laid the slight woman on the bed. I kissed her cheek. Denise kissed her lips gently before following me to our bedroom.

Denise removed her makeup as I brushed my teeth. I checked that my pistol was in the nightstand and out of its holster. The shockwave was under the bed pointed towards the chest of drawers. Denise walked out of the bathroom naked and crawled into bed. We were both exhausted from the long, emotionally draining day, so we didn't make love, but the skin-on-skin contact was very comforting. I turned out the light and Denise sprawled across me to lay her head on my shoulder. I kissed her before offering a short prayer, "God in Heaven, please protect us."

Denise muttered, "Amen." I think she fell asleep after three breaths. My awareness slowly faded.

☙❧

A DEEP BASSO BARK WAKES ME. I FINALLY FIGURE OUT ONE OF THE dogs is alerting us. I grab the Shockwave from under the bed and look out the bedroom window. I ghost out and cross the hall to look out my office window. Remus is looking out toward the road with a low growl.

I murmur, "Good boy, Remus." I drop so my head is the same height as his and look out the window. There is a big Dodge Ram pickup parked on the road next to the big elm tree on the north side of the yard. I see two figures, one of which is smoking. I back away from the window to find a naked Denise holding her M4.

"Two guys in a pickup on the road," I tell her. "That's well inside the range for slugs."

"I've got double-aught loaded, which should work at that distance. Slugs would be better," she says. "Let me get your VR80 and a couple magazines of slugs."

Her silhouette vanishes. I quietly make my way to Aliyah's room. Harry is standing with his muzzle on the windowsill. I think it's Harry. Muffy has white socks, and I don't see them.

I hear Denise call out, "Marc."

"Aliyah's room," I whisper.

Aliyah takes note of my presence at that point. She bounds off the bed and wraps her arms around me. "I'm scared, Marc."

"Me too, sweetie. That doesn't mean we won't kick their asses or even kill them if needed, okay?" She nods. "If the time to fight arrives, your warrior woman will come back out and your fear will be held in check. You will fight despite the fear." I feel her silky hair on my bare chest as she nods.

Parts of me are even more aware that I'm naked, holding Aliyah in what appears to be a very thin nightdress. Firm points of breast poke into my torso.

Aliyah asks as Denise walks in, "Marc, are you naked?"

"Uh...yeah," I admit bashfully. "Just don't turn on the lights, and you won't notice."

Denise giggles, "If you keep holding each other like that for long, she's going to notice, Marc."

Aliyah backs away, and Denise hands me a tac vest with pockets filled with shotgun magazines. I pull it on and she tells me, "The bottom two are slugs, the top two are double-aught buckshot. Here's the weapon, it's cleared and locked open."

I use my fingers to confirm as I watch the road. Denise hands me a magazine. "Slugs."

I give Denise a kiss and quietly ascend the stairs. I hear a canine whine following me. I take position low on the dormer window and look out. Buster snuggles next to me and looks out the window. The guy inhales whatever he is smoking, which lights his face in the glow. It's not enough to see features, just that it's a white guy.

I see the other guy start to creep forward. He's going slow, so it's hard to follow him. I think the motion sensor on the security light will still pick him up in another ten yards.

I slowly raise the window. The screen won't slow down a slug, but I may have to fire a second round. I get myself ready to fire. Just as I settle, I detect a faint red and blue flashing glow from the south. It gets brighter rapidly, and the figure crawling gets up and runs back to the truck. The smoker joins him. I see the crawling guy pull off night vision goggles as he runs to the truck. He trips over a root off the elm tree, but doesn't fall. The truck tears off down the road, and some sort of police car follows them less than half a minute behind them.

I call out, "Denise, turn on the front light."

After a short wait, she does, and the lawn looks all clear. I close the window, and Buster leads the way downstairs. There is light coming from the master bedroom to light the way. I see Denise pulling on a lightweight, white cotton robe that she frequently wears over her poet shirt or, like now, when she just wants a little cover to keep her naked-ness from catching a chill.

I clear the weapon, and she puts it back in the safe. I take off the vest and hang it. Denise hugs me, and I kiss her hungrily. I tell her, "I'm awake now."

Denise's hands grab my rapidly filling cock. Her eyes twinkle as she says, "I know how to make you sleepy."

"I better go empty my bladder first, Love. I'll get us a couple glasses of water too. I forgot to before bed," I tell her ruefully. "I'll meet you in bed."

I turn around to find Aliyah staring at my naked body - mostly below the waist. The light in the bedroom makes her voluminous, thin, cotton nightgown look nearly transparent. Her dark hair is loose, cascading down her shoulders to rest on her perky breasts. Those breasts are draped by the thin fabric, and there is a very visible shadow of her dark nipples and a very thick, dark bush.

I try desperately not to smack her with my now rigid cock as I slide past her through the doorway. I look back to see Aliyah facing Denise. I mime "Oh my God!" toward Denise and fan my face with my hand. Denise gives me away with a giggle, but I'm already marching down the hall, dodging all four excited huge dogs.

I call over my shoulder, "Aliyah, do you want one, too?"

"Yes, please," she answers distractedly.

I fill three water glasses and march back to the bedroom, carefully holding the three water glasses. Aliyah is now wrapped in an embrace with Denise, kissing her slowly but with definite passion. I slide by them and set the glasses on Denise's nightstand, carry one around the bed to my nightstand, and go pee. I come back to the bedroom, to find Aliyah backing toward the door as Denise walks toward me bashfully.

"Good idea," she says before kissing me and breezing past into the bathroom.

I look at our guest. "Are you staying, Aliyah?"

She looks at me like a deer caught in the headlights of an oncoming semi-truck. Her focus drops below my waist and locks on.

"I'll pull some pants on if you are, so you're not too uncomfort-able," I say and quickly pull out one of the few pairs of flannel pajama shorts I own from the dresser. I hold it in front of my genitalia, and Aliyah blinks like she's waking up from hypnosis. I turn around and step into the shorts. I pull out a t-shirt and pull that on, too.

Denise kisses me as my face emerges from the t-shirt. She murmurs, "Sorry, Love."

I wink at her and turn to face Aliyah. "For what, kissing that beautiful woman that obviously desires you? I don't blame you for that. If she wanted me like that, I'd kiss her too."

Aliyah looks scandalized and turns to leave. "I need to go to bed."

Denise sorrowfully watches her disappear down the hall. I whisper in her ear. "Would you like to tuck her in?"

Denise's face whips to look at me. "Really?"

"Denise, we have discussed this. I know you love me. I know you love Aliyah. Your love for her is different than your love for me, and the physical expression of it is likely a different experience for you. She needs you. Go. Go confidently in there to show her how much you love her - however that manifests," I tell her before gently kissing her.

"Goodnight, Marc," she says. She gives me a passionate kiss and slides out of my arms. She detours to grab the two water glasses before following Aliyah down the hall.

I check that the Shockwave and my pistol are in place before I pull the covers up. Buster bounds up onto the bed. I cock an eyebrow at him. "If you slobber on Denise's pillow, you'll have to sleep in the garage."

Buster whimpers like he understands and settles on the foot of the bed with his muzzle facing the door.

"You're a good boy, Buster," I assure the beast as I turn out the lights. His tail beats on my legs, but a wave of fatigue hits me as the adrenaline leaves my body. I drop off quicker than I thought I would.

※ 10 ※

THE SHERIFF VISITS

I wake up at seven with a canine face staring into mine. From the flash of white on its brindle chest I identify the correct Cuon. "Good morning, Muffy. How are you this morning, girl?"

She cocks her head at me as though she's processing my words. "Did you take good care of my ladies last night?" That earns me a kiss - a large, wet canine tongue across my entire face.

I push her away. "Okay, okay, okay," I grouse as I sit up. "I suppose you're hungry." The big dog chuffs quietly. "Fine. Go to the kitchen. I'll meet you there."

I get up, pee, and wash my face to clean the dog slobber from my face.

I pull on a pair of jeans over my pajama boxers, tuck my holster into the waistband, and slide my feet into my slippers. I grab my glass and head down the hall. I stop and backtrack to check...yep, Denise's pistol is in her nightstand. I pick it up and take it to Aliyah's room.

I knock gently on Aliyah's bedroom door. Hearing no response I slowly enter the room to find both ladies asleep facing the door. Harry looks over his shoulder at me before laying his head back onto his paws. Denise is spooned around Aliyah, and both ladies' naked shoulders are peaking out above the quilt. I gently place Denise's pistol on the nightstand.

Denise's eye's pop open, and I hold a finger to my lips. She flashes me a brilliant smile. I mime a gun with my thumb and index finger and point to the nightstand. She raises her head and nods. Then she cocks her head to beckon me closer. I lean over Aliyah and kiss Denise gently. She winks at me as I pull away.

Aliyah chooses that moment to wake up. She looks at me with a startled expression. I blow a kiss at her. She smiles shyly, so I lean in to kiss her forehead. I feel a hand slide up my back to squeeze me momentarily before I pull back to leave the ladies to wake up slowly. Aliyah gives me a tentative smile, and Denise flashes me one that is brilliant - filled with joy and love.

Muffy is sitting attentively in the hallway. "Whatsamatter, girl? You think daddy forgot about feeding you? Does your tummy think your throat was cut? Let's get you fed."

The huge dog gets up and bolts for the kitchen. I drain my water glass and set it on the counter. Muffy sticks her head back in the dog door to see what's keeping me.

I step out into the garage and get the big bucket of dog food out of the cabinet. I'm surprised to see all the bowls are empty. Normally, I fill the huge dog bowls every morning, but they're usually one-quarter to half-full the next morning. Remembering the opossum in the machine shed, I whisper to the big dog. "Muffy! Hunt."

Muffy looks at me quizzically and then starts sniffing the ground. She starts growling as she crawls under the workbench and sticks her nose behind the recycle barrel. I pull the barrel away from the wall, and another opossum dashes out and through the dog door of the garage to the yard.

I guess I shouldn't have tried to save money on that one. I will have to see if I can firm it up. If not, I'll have to replace it with one like I have on the house. I need to figure out how it got into the machine shed, too.

I fill all of the dog bowls. The five gallon bucket is getting low, so I fill it from the huge bag. Denise can handle the big bag, but this way it will be easier if she is the one feeding the dogs.

I fill the big water bowl in the garage before filling the one next to the door on the back porch.

I shake off the chill as I wash my hands and get started on breakfast. I grab bacon, eggs, frozen spinach, onion, and Boursin cheese. Remus and Buster hurry past for their own breakfast.

I am about to cut open the bacon, when I remember the dietary restrictions of Aliyah's faith. I put it back in the fridge, and find some leftover turkey bacon and leftover steak. I start pulling breakfast together.

I have turkey bacon fried and drying on napkins. The spinach is just about done with its sautée with onions when Aliyah appears in the kitchen. Harry slides past her to join the others outside for breakfast.

Aliyah walks closer to me hesitantly. She's back in that provocative nightgown with her hair uncovered. I'm definitely enjoying the view. I wash my hands and step around the counter, opening my arms to her. She rushes forward and hugs me.

"Thank you," she murmurs.

I tell her, "You have nothing to thank me for, Aliyah."

She looks up and tells me, "Denise said you recommended that she tuck me in."

I nod. "I did, but Denise is an adult. She chooses her own path. I just hope that she always chooses a path that is with me."

"Me too," Aliyah says shyly.

I lean down and gently kiss her lips. I half-expected to taste Denise on her, but there is no trace. I kiss her forehead and pull her close. "I think you're stuck, Sweetie. The odds of you getting rid of either of us are rather low."

She looks up again and smiles. Her eyes are dancing with joy. "Good," she murmurs huskily and pulls my face down to hers. Her eyes close, and her lips part as she presses a kiss to my mouth. I open my mouth as her tongue presses in and I caress it with my own. I caress her back down to the top of her buttocks and back.

I release her mouth and her eyes open. "Wow," she mutters.

"Wow is right!" Denise explains as she joins us in her robe. "You two look hot together. I should probably be jealous, but I'm excited instead." She wraps us both in a hug and kisses me first. She releases me and wraps Aliyah in her arms to devour her mouth like she just did mine.

I chuckle as I step back into the kitchen. I start breaking eggs as I share my observation, "So you two had a good time last night?"

Both ladies flush slightly before giggling, "Ye-e-es..."

I join their laughter. Denise says, "You'd think as much time as you've spent using your mouth and fingers on me, I would have had a better idea of what to do."

"You were great!" Aliyah blurts out. She shyly adds, "I didn't have any idea of where to start."

I tell them both, "That sounds like my wedding night, Aliyah. We were both virgins. I'd seen enough porn to understand some of the mechanics, but that's not the same as being confident. I discovered that as long as the emotional connection is there, then the rest of it will work itself out. From looking at the two of you, I'd say you have a good start."

Aliyah has a distant look. She says, "I have a lot of things to think about. Everything I want from Denise is not condoned by my faith. What I am currently dreaming of is not condoned by the law." She looks at me with a conspiratorial grin. "I am also curious about the taste of bacon and why it is forbidden. It smells sooo gooood."

"You almost found out this morning," I confess. "I had bacon out instead of turkey bacon. I caught it in time, but it was close."

Denise says, "I'm sure it comes from the Jewish faith. It's the parent of both Islam and Christianity. The Jewish folks eschew pork because pigs are essentially scavengers. A pig in the wild will eat dead things, mushrooms, and feces, which is plenty of reason to consider them 'unclean.' Additionally, they are prone to a variety of parasitic worms. Theoretically, modern, farm-grown pork shouldn't be a problem unless they are 'free range,' but the stigma remains in the dogma."

Remus bolts in through the dog door and jumps up onto his hind feet to look out the window. He growls, so I hurry to look out the window. "It's the Sheriff. Go ahead and change. No naked battles today."

Denise kisses me quickly and disappears down the hall. Aliyah bites her lip and turns to go. "Get back here and kiss me, young lady." She turns back with a grin and kisses me quickly before running down the hall. I enjoy the view for a moment, and then pull on my ropers without socks. Denise appears in yoga pants and a sweater with her pistol in one hand and the Shockwave in the other.

I see Sheriff Escola walk by the big picture window as Denise takes up position. I chamber a round as we hear a knock on the door. I unlock the door as the Sheriff calls out, "Call off your dogs!" He sounds a little flustered.

I open up the door, keeping the small shotgun hanging by my leg. "Come in, Sheriff."

He walks in and looks back at the dogs. "They're new."

Remus walks in from the dining room and growls. I command, "Remus, jump" The big dog drops to the ground and lays his head on his paws, watching the sheriff.

"Jesus!" he exclaims. "How many dogs did you get?" That's when Harry, Muffy, and Buster all choose to run into the living room. Harry 'jumps' in front of the hallway - Aliyah must be close. He has taken ownership of her. Muffy lays down next to Denise and Buster drops down next to his lifetime buddy.

"Just four," I say innocently. "Originally I got Remus and Buster." They raise their heads at the sound of their names. "A breeder-trainer was trying to offload some of his experiments, which is how Harry and Muffy came to join us. They are all very loving and obedient dogs."

He notes the small shotgun along my leg. "Apparently dogs aren't all you've been shopping for."

"Yeah," I admit. "I may need a rifle, too. I've been putting that off."

The sheriff removes his hat and scratches his short black hair before nodding to Denise, who is now sitting in the recliner with her pistol next to her hand. He says, "Ms. Schneider."

"Sheriff," Denise replies sweetly. She waves him to an armchair across from hers. "Please have a seat."

As he starts to move I say, "We should go to the kitchen. I've got stuff on the stove. Would you like a cup of coffee, Sheriff." I lead the way into the kitchen, and Aliyah emerges from the hallway in jeans, a long, shapeless, light blue tunic, and hijab. She did take the time to put on makeup with heavy kohl under her eyes.

Aliyah follows me into the kitchen, and Denise and the sheriff follow behind. Harry stays where he's at. Remus and Muffy go outside, and Buster parks himself in front of the door to the garage.

I put the Shockwave on top of the refrigerator and stir the contents of the skillet. Aliyah pours a cup of coffee and sets it in front of the sheriff. Denise does the introductions. "Sheriff Eskola, this is my best friend, Aliyah Sadduzai. Aliyah, this is Osage County Sheriff Michael Eskola. He called the Topeka police to find you after we were attacked."

Aliyah smiles pleasantly. "Thank you for saving my life, Sheriff. I hope you never have to do that again. Would you like sugar or milk for your coffee?"

The sheriff is entranced by Aliyah. He says, "Ms. Saduzzai, your accent acts like a blender on my brain. I drink my coffee black. Thank you."

Aliyah smiles and pours another cup, preparing it to Denise's specification. She places it in front of my fiancé before putting another pot on. I start cracking eggs. I set the big cast iron skillet I used for the turkey bacon into the oven to preheat it. Then I whip up the eggs with some herbs and spices as the sheriff starts to talk.

"Someone broke Joseph Connolly out of jail last night. We got some video of them, but it's not good enough for our facial recognition. The FBI task force is running it through their machines."

Denise says, "May I see it?"

The sheriff pulls out his phone and plays a video. Denise shakes her head prettily. She says, "No. I'm pretty sure he was at my wedding, but I don't recall his name. I think he's a Morrisey from Salina, but I'm not certain." The sheriff shows her another one. "That one is Michael Connolly," Denise says decisively.

The sheriff shrugs. "With the quality of the images, it was a long shot. I'm surprised you identified even one of them. I'll pass your opinion on to the task force. Regardless, there is a five-state APB out on Joseph. We got the other guys on video too, but they all wore balaclavas."

"What does APB mean?" Aliyah asks.

The sheriff gets all googly-eyed. He answers, "All points bulletin, ma'am. I thought everyone knew that with all the cop shows on TV."

She shrugs coquettishly. "I rarely watch television. I like Hallmark Channel. It does not seem so depraved as much of the other programming."

I have to admit, her alto voice with its Pakistani-English accent is lovely to listen to. I shred some cheddar cheese into the bowl with the eggs, crumble the turkey bacon into it, and then scoop the sautéed spinach and onions into it.

I continue working as I tell the sheriff, "We had visitors last night." I chop up the leftover steak into small bits and dump it into the bowl. The mixture is pretty thick. The alarm for the stove goes off to indicate it has reached 350 degrees Fahrenheit.

The sheriff responds as I set the steaming skillet on the stove top. "Yeah, about that. I had one of those 'gut feelings,' so I sent a deputy by here last night. He saw a pickup racing away as he pulled up to your place and pursued."

I pour the egg mixture in the skillet, stir it, and break up the block of Boursin into small pieces that I drop into the mixture.

The sheriff says. "He followed them west, but lost sight of them at the old Highway 75. The deputy picked north, but he could see that he chose the wrong direction as he crested the hill running down into the Wakarusa river valley." I cover the skillet and put it in the oven as he continues. "He backtracked back down to Carbondale, but found no sign of them. In hindsight, it is easier to lose a tail in an urban environment, but Carbondale is so small I wouldn't think of it as an urban environment either."

I respond, "Honestly, they could have pulled into that trailer park just south of Hooterville and shut off the lights with just a couple of minutes of lead."

"Yeah," the sheriff agrees. "He didn't think about the trailer park. Honestly, I didn't either. He was gone in the other direction for quite a while, so that could have worked. Or they could have raced down to Carbondale, and taken the US-75 back toward Topeka from there.

Either way, the deputy went back and took up surveillance just south of your yard, parking in the treeline. He left at sun-up."

I nod as I ponder all that. Eventually, I say, "Sheriff, they have tried to kill or intimidate Aliyah three times. They've come to the house twice that I know of. Last night one of them had night vision goggles and was crawling toward the house." I pause to collect my thoughts. "Sheriff, if they come back, I am not going to be polite to them. Some of them will be hurt severely. It will make Sean and Joseph's experience look like a cakewalk."

"Sean died, Mr. Hough," he replies with a deadpan expression.

I chew on that for a moment. "Two dead Connollys. How many more are out there?"

"More than we want to deal with," Denise says. "On the positive side, I understand that the ones in the other branch of the family aren't psychotic at all. Actually, Daniel's baby sister, Rosemarie, is a sweetie, too."

Aliyah says shyly, "As much as I hate to admit it, that psychotic prat dying does cheer me somewhat."

I put two slices of bread in the toaster before asking, "How many of your people were hurt in the breakout, Sheriff?"

"Two," he replies quietly. "They killed the dispatcher and the deputy on duty guarding the cells. I had light coverage because we only had the one prisoner. The two night deputies were out on patrol."

"You've been up all night?" Denise asks. He nods and hides his face behind a sip from his coffee cup.

Denise says, "Aliyah, shall we set the table?" She holds up four fingers. Aliyah and I both nod.

I ask, "How is the deputy that Sean attacked doing?" I keep feeding bread into the toaster and get out another stick of butter.

He nods and responds. "He's home. He comes back to work on Monday. Miss Sadduzai's father cleared him for duty."

He balks as Aliyah sets a flatware down in front of him. "Oh, I can't stay for breakfast."

I hand Aliyah a plate full of toast before I pull the skillet out of the oven.

Denise pats him on the shoulder as she says, "Baloney, Sheriff.

You've been up all night for a tragic event. You didn't have to come up here, you could have called. We are going to feed you so you have the energy to take care of whatever comes next."

I plate the frittata, and Denise puts the plates on the table while Aliyah pours small glasses of orange juice. I grab a couple of mugs for coffee and fill one for Aliyah and myself. Aliyah takes the pot from me and refills Denise and Sheriff Eskola. The frittata is plenty for four people.

We all dig into breakfast, and the conversation dries up. After the meal, I start clearing the table.

The sheriff jokes, "Mr. Hough, you're going to make someone a great wife someday."

"Mine!" Denise exclaims and shows him her engagement ring.

Aliyah jokes, "He is quite handy, Denise. As your BFF, I am certain you will loan him to me when I need help."

The ladies laugh as I shrug and say, "I've pretty much always worked from home. When I was married before, my wife worked as a teacher, so I took care of most of the domestic duties. She helped with cleaning on the weekend, but I tried to take care of everything so we could hike, bike, ski, or whatever on the weekends."

"Makes sense," he nods. "Since my wife and I both work, I end up doing a lot more cleaning than I ever figured I would."

I chuckle, "I get the feeling you are as well trained as a husband as I am."

"And I reap rewards," Denise laughs. "And Aliyah does too since she's staying with us."

Aliyah smiles and blushes as she looks at me.

"Well, I need to get back on the road," the sheriff says as he stands. "Thank you all for your kindness. I will have a unit posted on the road tonight."

"If you want to have them park in the driveway, we could do that. Just have your dispatcher call in advance. I'm going to set the security light to always on rather than motion detection," I tell him.

"If my deputy parks where they were last night it will be hard to see his unit," he says. "I'll call you personally if that changes. Here's my card." He gives us each one.

I grab the Shockwave and walk him to the door. "Get some sleep, Sheriff. You need to stay sharp."

He pauses and looks back at me. "I want you as a deputy, Mr. Hough. With the increase in drug traffic we get overwhelmed sometimes. Having an experienced, part-time deputy could be helpful."

I just look at him for a moment. "I'm a writer, Sheriff. Plus, I've got my hands full protecting my family. Come talk to me after this is all over."

The sheriff nods, crawls into his pickup, and drives away. I close and lock the doors.

Denise hugs me fiercely. "If you become a part-time deputy, I will too. You're not going out there without me."

"You would have to go through the police academy, Denise. As a former, MP, I wouldn't - especially as a reserve deputy," I explain. She frowns at me until I add, "Don't worry, Love. I have no intention of putting on a uniform again."

Denise smiles, "Good. I like the idea of having a house husband who cooks for me and fucks my brain out at night."

"Allah have mercy, Denise," Aliyah gasps. She's obviously blushing, but Denise giggles and devours my mouth.

I squeeze her firm ass and she gasps, "Why, Sir! I do believe you are fondling my bum!"

"Well Pet, I most certainly hope I am," I reply with a shocked tone. "Otherwise, I am being exceedingly forward with Miss Sadduzai. I think we would both be rather beside ourselves."

I hear Aliyah gasp before she starts laughing hysterically. I feel a small hand land on mine, and it squeezes my hand and Denise's tushy.

I gasp, "Ms. Sadduzai! Are you holding my hand?"

Aliyah giggles, and Denise gasps. "Sir. Methinks the trollop is also squeezing my bum!"

I look to the side to find Aliyah's silken hair unbound, and her hijab is hanging around her neck while she laughs in a carefree manner. For just one short moment, the cares of murderous, criminal, rogue policemen are forgotten.

Aliyah wraps her arms around us both as we ride the wave of laughter. As we smile at each other, Aliyah sighs. She says, "I suppose we should practice marksmanship."

I look at Denise and nod. "Yes, Aliyah. Grab your crossbow."

She kisses each of us briefly on the cheek and dashes off.

Denise observes, "She took off her hijab just for you."

I chew on that for a moment. "Yes. I am honored that she trusts me that much." I brush my lips across Denise's. "What are you up to, my love?"

"Me?" she asks innocently. Her eyes sparkle with mischief. "Sir, whatever could I be up to? Hmmm?"

I shake my head and ask, "Shall we get ready, Love?" Denise nods, and we return to the bedroom to put on clothes to go outside.

11

VISITORS IN THE NIGHT

We spent the afternoon down the slope from the house in the hay barn. I put the target and an old broom in the back of my truck and drove it down to the hay barn. Once there, I placed it against a stack of large hay bales.

Denise and I worked with Aliyah on her marksmanship with the crossbow for about an hour. By the end of that period, she put the twenty bolts in a group in the bullseye or tightly around it at fifteen feet. After that, we had her work on her quick-fire technique. I added swinging the broom at her to make her duck or dodge to hit her target. Her accuracy suffered initially, but it appeared to improve quickly as she got used to the idea. Denise would periodically push on her shoulder to mix it up; however, Aliyah had already adapted to deal with mild threats. She just rolled with it and kept hitting the target.

After Denise and I were satisfied with Aliyah's ability with the crossbow, we hugged her fiercely and told her how proud of her we were. She blushed at the praise, but she seemed to appreciate it as well.

At that point, I gave her a basic firearms safety lecture. She parroted back the correct advice for different scenarios before Denise primed her on the Ruger .22 pistol.

Aliyah struggled with the pistol. I had her rotate back and forth between the crossbow and the pistol, but the basic problem was that she was afraid of the firearm whereas she just viewed the crossbow as a dart-throwing device. After switching back and forth for about an hour, she had firmer control of the pistol, but the fear remained. We had her clear the weapon before we consoled her with another hug.

After a glass of water, we all sat down and taught Aliyah how to clean her weapon. My inner army sergeant came out to visit, but Aliyah just smiled and kept at it until the weapon passed muster.

We made dinner as the sun approached the horizon. The dogs alerted during early evening twilight. I stepped out on the front porch and looked down the road to the south to see a Sheriff's Deputy car parking in the ditch next to the trees. The deputy got out of the car and scanned his surroundings. Noticing me on the front porch, he waved and got back into his unit. I waved back before I went back inside and texted the Sheriff to let him know his deputy arrived.

We were on edge for the rest of the evening. We spent the time familiarizing Aliyah with how the other weapons in the house work, followed by a group hug on the couch. We went to bed just before ten o'clock. Denise and I made love quietly and gently, but even that didn't allow us to fall asleep easily. We eventually got up to put on clothes - black yoga pants and a sports bra for Denise, dark blue waffle shirt and dark grey cargo pants for me. We lay in each other's arms and eventually drifted off.

SOMETHING JUST WOKE ME. I DON'T KNOW WHAT IT IS, BUT something caused me to bolt up wide awake and reach for my weapon. Muffy runs in and looks out the window by Denise's side of the bed. Denise slides out of bed and squats on the floor to pull on her sweater, and I pull on some lugged sole slip-on shoes. I clip on the M&P and grab the Shockwave while I scan outside from the side of the window.

The lights from the deputy are flashing. There is a pickup parked behind the deputy's car and I see figures crawling through the fence into our pasture to the south.

I command, "Muffy, jump." The huge dog drops like a sack of flour and whimpers.

Denise opens the safe and says, "You'll get your chance, girl. Patience."

"Two coming through to the south pasture. They'll probably come through the gate into the yard. Both have NVGs," I report.

"Huh?" Denise grunts.

"Night vision goggles," I clarify. "Sorry, Love. I fear I'm reverting to Afghanistan."

I call the Sheriff. He answers, "WHAT?"

"Attack in progress. I'm not sure how many yet, but it looks like they got your deputy. I see carbines and night vision goggles on the two I can see," I report as I pull on my tac-vest.

"Same load as before, Love," Denise murmurs as she hands me my Glock on the thigh holster.

"*Shit! They attacked the station, too. I'll send the Carbondale cops to you and try to get some more state cops to you,*" the sheriff growls. "*Just try to hold out for help.*"

I strap on the gun belt, secure the holster to my thigh, and clip the M&P to the back of the gunbelt. I hear a burst of silenced gunfire and a quiet shriek from Aliyah.

"Roger. Gotta run, Sheriff," I drop the phone.

I strap on the Glock and advance as the light in Aliyah's room flashes on and off. I hear a male voice curse. The return of darkness is followed by the sound of Aliyah's .22 firing repeatedly and a growling dog.

I call out softly, "I'm behind you, Aliyah." I advance into the room and see a body hanging through the window. I put the pistol to his head and check the hanging right arm for a pulse - nothing. I grab his carbine. The selector is past 'semi' position, which would mean 'three-round burst' on an M-16. *Interesting.* I pull the guy farther into the room, pull off his tac vest and body armor, and toss the armor to Aliyah.

I tell her, "Put that on." I see a crew cab truck pull into the drive-way, and four guys in body armor get out of it with carbines.

I aim at the head of the closest with the silenced carbine from

Aliyah's attacker. My target falls against the truck, so I fire again - aiming for his legs. The other three start running as I scan to the next closest. I pull the trigger as they return fire. I duck down as the glass shatters around me.

I grab the pistol from the corpse hanging from the window and crawl behind the bed with Aliyah. It feels like my Glock.

"Are you okay?" I ask. I check the controls to confirm they are the same. *Yep, it's a Glock.*

"Scared to death, but I have managed to not wet myself," she replies with black humor.

"That's better than some guys I served with. You're not hit?" I ask.

"No, Marc," she says. I notice her night dress is pooled on the floor, but she does have the armor on.

She crawls to her suitcase and pulls out a pair of dark pants. I drop the magazine as I catch a glimmer of her naked ass before she pulls on the pants. I clear the new pistol. I pick up the round and stuff it into the magazine as Aliyah joins me. I give the Glock and magazine to Aliyah. She looks at them, loads the magazine, and chambers a round.

I tell her, "That packs a bigger punch than your .22. Keep them both with you." I see her nod in the low light.

I hear four blasts from Denise's shotgun out of my office. I hurry back down the hall towards her with the carbine and Shockwave in my hands when I hear a deep booming sound on the back door. I hear breaking glass as Denise commands, "Muffy, hunt." I turn toward the front of the house

The baying of Remus and Buster quiets just before I hear another boom and the door hitting the wall. I step into the little hall across from Aliyah's bedroom that leads to the bathroom and laundry. Denise slides in behind me, and calls out, "Harry." The big dog sticks his head out of the room. Denise grabs him and leads him to my office before commanding, "Harry, hunt!"

She murmurs to me, "I'm in our bedroom doorway. I got both of the guys coming through the pasture gate. I shot them in the legs and got a head shot on one of them."

"Good plan, Love," I murmur back as I see laser sights painting the living room walls. A guy in body armor and NVGs scans his carbine down the hall, and I shoot him with the silenced carbine. Unfortunately, I reverted to army training and shot center of mass.

The attacker laughs as he falls, and one of his buddies steps into the hallway and starts spraying rounds down the hallway. I duck back and pick up the Shockwave. I stick it out with my left hand, aim low, and squeeze the trigger. As the weapon roars, I feel a burn across my left shoulder.

The first guy is getting up on his knees as I rack a fresh round into the chamber and ghost forward. I point my red dot at his mouth and pull the trigger. His head explodes. I hear the dogs growling as a masculine voice whimpers.

"Remus, Buster, heel!," I command.

The guy moans, "You shot my balls!"

I see him on the floor in the faint light. I whisper. "Hey!"

He raises his head, and I shoot him in the face. I strip his vest and body armor off and drag his corpse to the broken door. I push it closed and lay his body in front of it. I do the same to his buddy. I give Denise a vest. I guard while she puts it on. When she is done, she guards while I pull on the last one.

I tell her, "There were four in the last truck. Assuming the same number in the first truck, there should be at least three of them out there unless you killed 'em both."

Denise responds, "I saw a car pull in as you were barricading the door. I only saw two more guys get out of it."

"Fuck," I respond. "Carbondale and state police are supposed to be on the way. I can't hear sirens, but that might be from impairment after the gun fire."

"Stay here," she says.

She shuffles back and returns with my VR80, my phone, and wired headset. She says, "Getting shot SUCKS!"

"You're hit?" I'm frantic.

"Through the muscle in my leg. It isn't bleeding much, and it somehow managed to miss the bone. I cinched a belt around it. I'll be okay," she assures me.

I hug her briefly. She hands me my phone gear. "I started a group call with you, Aliyah, and me. Put in your earbuds," she orders.

"Just one," I tell her.

"Both, Marc!" she orders. "Put your range headset on over it. You'll be able to hear us, and anything around you if you keep the volume on the protectors to at least fifty percent."

"Yes, ma'am," I answer and follow orders.

She says, "Good, Sir," while patting my shoulder. I hiss at the contact on the graze wound on my shoulder. She gasps, "Shit, you're hit, too."

"I think it's just a graze," I tell her. "Let's finish this." I push more rounds into the Shockwave until the magazine is full.

Denise swaps me for my VR80. She says, "Buckshot." I check both of my pistols are in place and roll to my feet. I grab the carbine and pull the magazine from it. The corpses at the door appear to have the same weapons. I put a fresh magazine in the carbine.

I say into my microphone, "Commo check, Denise."

"I can hear you," comes through my headset.

"Commo check, Aliyah."

I hear, "Allie is here. I can hear you."

I chuckle, "Roger, Allie. You two stay in this internal hallway. Retreat to the basement if you have to. Upstairs is the last choice unless another vehicle arrives. Then snipe them from the upstairs window."

"Got it," Denise says. She gives me a quick kiss, and I head for the garage.

I call, "Remus, stay. Buster, come." The big Bull Mastiff whines. I scratch his ear and tell him, "Remus, protect Denise and Aliyah." The big dog looks at Denise and jumps to lie at her feet.

I hear a guy scream in the yard as I slink out into the garage. His cries quiet to a gurgle. I command, "Buster, hunt." The big Rottweiler pushes out the dog door on the north side of the garage.

I'm about to follow when the garage door begins to rise slowly. I think for just a moment. I check behind the recycle bin, and see the opossum laying there. I push the muzzle of my shotgun down on it's head and grab it by the scruff with my left. It starts to hiss and spit.

I grab the ax off the wall and hook the light cable for the garage door opener out of the socket with it. The light doesn't come on, so I count it as a win. The door reaches the top of its travel to reveal two guys with NVG's sitting on top of their heads and carbines hanging from slings.

They chuckle quietly at some shared joke and step into the garage.

I throw the opossum at one, and split the skull of the other with the ax. The other guy screams as the angry animal claws and bites his face. That's when Buster appears and mauls the guy's leg.

Buster's victim grabs his carbine. I chop the ax into his left shoulder and leave it sticking in his body to pick up my shotgun. I put the muzzle to his right elbow and pull the trigger. His arm falls to the ground, but I hear Buster whimper. I shoot the guy above his knee, which turns it to hamburger. Gotta love double-aught buckshot.

I check my dog. It appears Buster was shot in the left ham. I guide him to the garage so he doesn't get too much dirt in the wound. I kiss the top of his head and tell him, "Buster, jump."

"You're a good boy. Daddy's gonna go make all these evil fucks pay," I tell him.

He wags his tail as he lies there and whimpers. I tell him, "Buster, guard."

He chuffs and watches out the garage door.

I grab the carbine and ensure the selector is on 'semi.'

Denise reports, "The two guys from the car are heading toward the garage. I think they turned off the electricity at the pole."

"I'll get it, Love."

I grab NVGs from the guy that is dying slowly. I close my right eye and pull them on and ghost to the snowball bush outside the north garage exit. I take a prone position, sliding the shotgun to lay on my back. I see my two targets. I turn off the NVGs and remove them before I open my right eye. I sight on the slender guy with my borrowed carbine and squeeze the trigger twice. I pick up the other guy as he runs. I flip the selector back to auto, and squeeze the trigger twice. He fires back, but his aim is high. I'm able to get a clear shot of his head, and lead him enough for the burst to hit where I want.

"I think I got them both," I report.

Aliyah reports, "The first one for certain. The second one is still twitching. There's another one lying next to the truck. He appears injured. This night vision is handy."

"Try to keep your primary eye closed in case you have to take them off," I tell her. "I'm going to clear the east and south side of the house. You should have power shortly." Then I see the Cuons run around the house. I command, "Harry, Muffy, heel."

They dash to my side and sniff me eagerly. "Such good puppies. Yes. Daddy loves you, too." I take off around the east side and post Muffy as a guard on the house door in the garage.

Harry and I clear the east and south sides. I find the two guys Denise shot. One has an exploded head, the other looks like he bled out of wounds in his crotch and a torn throat. *'Note to self. Don't piss off the dogs!'* I go to the pole with the main service switch and turn the power back on. "Denise, do you have power?"

"Yes, Sir. The nightlight in the guest bath just lit," she answers.

A guy in body armor runs into the yard and yells, "What the fuck are you doing? Stick to the fucking plan!" Apparently he has mistaken me due to the body armor and NVG. He is coming at me fast but not running.

I say quietly, "Making sure we got them all."

The guys yells, "Use the fucking goggles." He's about five meters away. I quick-draw my Glock and double-tap him in the throat and face. I hurry forward and check for a pulse - nothing.

I hurry to the deputy's car. I call out, "Deputy! Marcus Hough approaching."

I hear a weak response. "Call for help! They attacked dispatch again!"

I open the car door and see him lying down across the console. "I called the Sheriff. Help is supposed to be on the way. Denise, call an ambulance. Deputy..."

"Crowley," he coughs.

"...Deputy Crowley has been shot three times. Once in each shoulder, and a third round went under his vest from his left armpit. He has blood bubbles on his lips, so I think they caught a lung. I'm going to try to carry him to the house."

"On it, Marc," Aliyah responds. "She's talking to the 911 operator."

I hear Aliyah relay everything to Denise as I grab the Deputy by his vest and pull him toward me.

I squat and pick him up in a fireman's carry. He's heavy, but I'm still on an adrenaline rush. "Allie, please open the front door and then get a blanket for the sofa," I say into the microphone on the headset.

"Right away, Sir." I smile wondering if she knows the connotation Denise uses with that title.

"We need a vet for Buster, too. He took a round in the ass," I report.

"Right away, Sir," Aliyah responds.

I step up through the open front door in time to see Aliyah run into the living room. I command, "Harry, guard." The big dog sits in the dining room facing the front door.

I carry Deputy Crowley into the living room and squat to deposit him on the sofa. I remove his gun belt and then the belt from his pants. Aliyah brings the first aid kit, and I pull off his vest and body armor and thread the belt under his armpits. Aliyah puts a clean gauze patch over the entry wound. I don't see an exit. I cinch the belt tightly across his chest to provide pressure.

The deputy moans, "Jesus!" I ease him to lie down on his left side to keep blood out of his hopefully healthy right lung.

Denise announces, "Ambulance is on its way. I see flashers getting closer from the south. They're going to send an emergency vet they use for the Topeka and Shawnee County K-9 units."

"Thanks, Love," I respond as I pull the blanket over the deputy. "Aliyah, let's get another blanket on him. Closet at the end of the hall. Then watch him. If his chest bulges, release the belt. I need to secure any living attackers and see if I can get Buster inside."

Aliyah kisses my lips gently, and I squeeze her slight body close. I notice she has a black hijab on. Girlfriend's turning into a ninja.

I release her and go to the garage. I turn on the light and command, "Muffy, heel." The big dog stands at my side as I go to check on Buster. He stands awkwardly. I kneel before him and hug him. I hook the leg of the injured buttock and lift it. "Just like that, Buster."

I can see the pain in my sweet dog's eyes. "I don't think it's fatal, buddy. A vet is on the way. Shall I carry you inside?" He acts embarrassed by the indignity of the idea. I tell him something I know he'll understand. "Buster, bed."

He chuffs and licks my face before hobbling on three legs into the house. I check the guy with amputations. He has a flashlight that I pilfer before I check his wounds. He has a very slight pulse. I grab zip ties and use them as a tourniquet for the stump of his arm and above his knee.

His buddy with the cleaved skull is done. Six dead, one wounded.

The two guys from the car are both dead. Eight dead, one wounded. The guy I first shot with the carbine isn't by the truck. I kneel next to the blood trail. I point and command, "Muffy, hunt."

She sniffs the trail and follows the blood trail across the yard. I jog to keep up. The blood trail angles across the driveway to the recently repaired mailbox. I look at the guy lying there weakly reaching for his sidearm. I shine the light in his face and say, "Hello, Joseph."

I toss his pistol into the driveway before I grab him by the back collar. He's got a taser, which I also claim. I drag Joseph facedown across the driveway and drop him on the grass. I tell Muffy, "Guard." The huge dog lies in front of the felon and watches him steadily. Smart dogs are a freakin' awesome.

A police car crawls up next to the deputy's car. I see another one coming down the road from the north as I remove the magazine from the carbine. One round left. I toss the magazine in the driveway and clear the chamber. I remove the upper receiver from the bottom and toss the parts to the driveway.

I walk toward the Carbondale policeman with my hands in the air. A searchlight shines at me, and I have to turn away from the glare. Focusing my eyes to the side and toward the ground, I continue.

I hear the cop yell, "Marcus Hough?"

I yell back, "Yes, officer."

I hear him mutter, "Holy shit," before he turns off the light. He talks into his radio, and the other unit slows.

I get close enough to say, "I moved the Deputy inside the house, and did some very poor first aid. An ambulance is on the way."

The officer walks out from behind his car door with his hand on his weapon. He looks familiar. I think he was a freshman when I was a high school senior. The officer removes his hand from his gun and asks, "What is that?"

I look where he is pointing before answering. "Are you talking about the dirtbag that keeps trying to kill me, or the huge dog guarding him?"

"That's a dog?" he asks incredulously.

"Yeah," I answered tiredly. "Let me walk you around the crime scene."

I see another unit coming from the south and three more from the north.

❦

WHEN THE UNITS ARRIVED, I DISCOVERED TWO OF THE ONES FROM the north and the one from the south were ambulances. I told the paramedics about the wounded in priority order - Deputy Crowley, the amputee, Denise, Joseph, and myself. They wanted to put Joseph higher than Denise, but I told them I wouldn't call the dog off Joseph until they'd taken care of Denise. Two crews went inside and one worked on 'amputee guy.' It didn't take long for Crowley's team and 'amputee guy's' teams to decide they needed an air medevac. They called it in, and the helicopter was supposed to be on station in twenty minutes. I was the only person present that knew how to set up a night landing zone, or 'LZ,' so one of the Carbondale cops followed me in his car to the pasture directly east of the house.

The policeman had both chemlights and flares. We marked the corners of the LZ with chemlights, and then I dug up the grass on the four corners of the LZ. The idea was that we would use flares without starting a brush fire. I got the corners prepped when the ambulance driver said the aircraft was inbound. The policeman and I lit traffic flares at the corners. He parked his vehicle with lights flashing at the south boundary as the aircraft approached. I noticed a lot more police cars in the yard than when I started the task. I recognized Agent Howell of the KBI and Sheriff Eskola walking around.

I walked a wide path around the helicopter as two teams of medics carried stretchers. I saw Denise holding Muffy by the collar, so the paramedics could attend Joseph. They ended up loading him on a stretcher and putting him on the helicopter, too. A state cop jumped into the aircraft just before it took off.

I went into the machine shed and pulled out drop cords and my two work lights to let the police see better. Theirs hadn't arrived yet, and I still had them in the machine shop for when Dad needed to repair equipment in a field. Rather than hooking up a generator, I just ran a drop cord out the garage window. Then the adrenaline crash hit me hard - the last thing I remembered was starting to shake and thinking *'That grass is getting really close!'*

I woke up on the couch with two paramedics tending to me, with Denise, Aliyah, and Sheriff Eskola all looking over their shoulders with various worried expressions.

I winked at the ladies, and Denise sighed heavily and shook her head slowly. "Don't scare me like that, Marcus!"

"Sorry, Love," I respond quietly. "I'm outta practice. I used to last for two-to-three hours before a crash, and then I just went to sleep."

The paramedic said, "That's essentially what you did. Between the blood loss and dehydration, I'm surprised you lasted as long as you did. I thought you were the least injured."

"I am," I told him.

Denise said, "I barely bled by comparison. If I had seen how blood-soaked your arm was, I would have insisted on you being seen after the deputy."

"His assessment wasn't off, ma'am," the other paramedic said. "Some first aid could have prevented some of the bloodloss. The real problem was he kept using it."

I lost focus for a moment before saying, "Compared to Afghanistan, this was a picnic."

"Tru dat," says the first paramedic as he slides a catheter in my arm. "You haven't lost enough blood to need a transfusion. Plasma and saline should take care of you. I'll put the saline in your other arm. We need to take you in for stitches."

The sheriff said, "Can you do that here? Maybe staples and a dressing. I need a deputy to go with me to my next stop. All the others close by are dead or injured. You up for it, sergeant?"

I looked at him for a long moment, and Denise and Aliyah started objecting.

The sheriff barked, "Ladies! Please hear me out." Both ladies stopped for a moment. The sheriff said, "Your fiancé is the only trained law enforcement officer available. Carbondale police can help, but they don't have the level of training of Mr. Hough. They would probably die. Look out there." He points toward the cluster around the vehicles and bodies. "He wounded two and killed eight of them. He's trained for this. I've got two state cops here to help."

"Um, Sheriff." He took a breath, and I continued. "Actually, Denise killed two of them, and Aliyah killed one of them. I only got five."

The sheriff closed his eyes for a moment before responding. "Good. Then they will be safe here with all these state and federal pencil pushers. One of my off-duty jailers followed the attackers in his personal truck after they left my office. He found their local headquarters. I've got Deputy Morgan on surveillance, but he's not officially on duty until Monday - light duty only after that. The jailer is covering another route in and out, but he's not been in the field in ten years. The rest of the house is either processing our office or on mandatory rest to cover tomorrow. I need another deputy."

"I'm not a deputy," I pointed out.

The sheriff held up a badge. "You will be as soon as they patch you up. When they were carting out the bodies from my office, I logged this badge to your name with the date and time of assignment. I need two witnesses, and I can clean up the rest of the paperwork tomorrow or Monday."

Denise gasped, "Marc, please! No!" Her strident plea caused Remus, Harry, and Muffy all to crawl closer to Denise. Buster whined from his bed.

I was inclined to go with her opinion until the sheriff said, "Michael and Seamus are both there. I'm surprised they haven't fled or come to join the party here."

Fear mixed with anger painted Denise's face. She patted the paramedic on the back and said, "Move!" She leaned in and kissed me passionately. She asked, "Can you do this?"

I nodded, "Yeah. I've done it before. I wasn't always worried about apprehending suspects at the time, but apprehending was the mission more often than not. I can handle it."

She caressed my face and looked lovingly in my eyes. Hers glistened with tears as she said, "If you can't safely apprehend them, put them in the ground." She wiped her eyes and said, "If you can manage it, I would really like to attend their executions."

"I will give you that gift, my Love," I told her. I looked at the paramedic. "Sutures are better than staples. Do you have any stimulants?"

The paramedic looked at me, "I can only give you a mild one."

I nodded. "That should be enough. Patch me up, Doc. I need to go to battle." I looked at the Sheriff. "I'm in."

Twenty minutes later, after getting put back together with a little added joy juice, I was on my feet without any catheters - my right hand in the air. Sheriff Eskola swore me in as a deputy of the Osage County Sheriff with the two paramedics and Agent Howell as his witnesses. Aliyah took video of the entire ceremony. Sheriff Eskola gave me Crowley's windbreaker and helmet. The helmet fit, but the jacket was a little short. We took a few minutes to prep my weapons. Denise had cleaned my VR80, and loaded the magazine and breach with double-aught buckshot - five rounds plus one in the chamber. Aliyah emptied and loaded the magazine for the Glock and ran a swab through the barrel. I cleared it and function-checked it before chambering a round and loading another into the magazine. I did the same with the M&P. Aliyah helped me hang my phone as a bodycam - duct tape and heavy household twine did the job

I got in the Sheriff's truck and pushed the helmet on my head. Remus and Harry jumped in the back. It turned out that we were driving to that trailer park about a mile and a half from the house on old Highway 75 - where the deputy lost our attackers last night. No lights. No sirens.

Sheriff Eskola pulled up next to a trailer house about half way into the trailer park from the highway and one lot off the dirt road. The two highway patrol cars that followed us pulled in behind us. One of them talked on the phone and quickly hung up. He pulled a shotgun and met us at the Sheriff's truck. He said, "That was the watch commander. Two more units are about a minute out." I noticed he had sergeant stripes.

The other patrolman joined us carrying a door ram. The sheriff told the sergean, "You cover the back door." He pointed at the other patrolman, "You and I hit the door with the ram."

He looked at me, "Deputy Hough, you lead the way on point."

I nodded, "Remus and Harry will go first, and I will enter with them and move to the center of the entryway. You two follow behind and clear left and right." They nodded.

Two more highway patrol cars pulled into the trailer park. The sergeant greeted them. We decided that one would cover the rear exit with the sergeant, one would cover the front door for anyone trying to slip by.

12

CLEANING UP

Everyone is in position. The sheriff and the patrolman are poised in front of the front door. I turn on the camera of my phone. I command the dogs. "Remus, Harry, heel." The dogs lean into my legs as the breach team swing the ram back. I put a hand on each of the dog's heads. They can feel that we're back in the shit.

The ram hits the door, and the door flies into the trailer. The officers get out of the way, and I whisper fiercely to the dogs. "Hunt." They launch through the door of the trailer. I hear a lot of voices cursing, shouting, and one of the men inside screaming. I pull my shotgun up to my shoulder and hurriedly follow the dogs yelling "Police! Freeze!" three times. I find seven men around an oval dining table with beers in hand.

One of the guys opens the back door and jumps out. I hear the officer in the back yell, "Freeze! On your knees!" Two of the men draw pistols. I shoot the one focusing on me. I shoot at his neck, and his neck turns to hamburger before I aim at the one pointing his gun at Harry. I shoot him in the arm, which knocks him to the ground. Harry pounces on him. Another guy pulls a pistol, he's raising it from behind his back. I shoot him in the bladder, and he drops like a stone. Double-aught buckshot is a wonder.

I yell again, "Police! Everyone freeze! I will not tell you again. I've got a round for each one of you, so lay on the ground if you want to live." Two guys drop to the ground as the sheriff and patrolman enter and break left and right. Another one reaches for a weapon on his belt, I rejoice inside as I shoot Seamus Connolly in the knee.

"Remus, guard," I call out. Remus runs out of the corridor to the right and stands over Seamus.

I hear the patrolman holler "Clear."

The last guy standing reaches across his torso as the patrol officer walks out. The perp whips his hand across his body.

Time slows as I raise my shotgun vertically with my left hand. I see a metallic object spinning towards me as my right hand drops to the Glock on my thigh. I deflect the knife with the shotgun barrel as I draw the pistol and fire it at the perfect moment. I see the hole appear in the center of his forehead just before I slide the pistol back into the hoster. My perception returns to normal speed as I raise the shotgun to firing position, and the guy drops dead to the floor.

I scan the room and call out, "Harry, guard!" The growling stops, and the sheriff and patrolman cuff the two guys that surrendered. I drop my shotgun down my back and remove the belt of the guy I shot in the bladder. I wrench the windbreaker out from under my weapon sling and roll it into a ball with the fleece lining facing out. I use the guy's belt to cinch the ball into his wound.

This guy is definitely a Connolly. I roll him over and use his own cuffs on him. The sheriff cuffs Seamus Connolly. I whip Seamus' belt off and use it as a tourniquet above his destroyed knee.

The patrolman calls out, "I need some help here."

I run over. Harry is guarding the suspect from the patrolman. "Harry, heel."

The huge dog bounds to my side, and the officer mutters, "Thanks."

I hold the wounded guy forward, bending him at the waist while the officer cuffs him despite having one arm hanging by a thread. I lay the guy back, and the officer pulls the guy's belt out of his pants. He offers it to me, and I thread the belt under the guy's armpit and tighten it until the blood flow slows.

The officer calls on his radio, "Send paramedics to the trailer park." He nods to me, and I stand.

"Remus, heel," I call. Remus joins Harry and me, and I lead them outside. I lean against the sheriff's truck and slowly slide to the ground. My dogs lay down on either side of me and rest their heads on my lap. I shut off the video and save it to Dropbox and Google Pictures.

The sheriff comes outside and kneels in front of me. "How're you holding up, Deputy Hough?"

"Feeling kind of rough, Sheriff. I think I ran out of go-juice. Can I go home now? It's a bit of a walk. It's going to take me a while." I respond.

The sheriff chuckles. He says, "Deputy Morgan is going to detour to drop you off on his way home."

I grin. "Thanks, Sheriff." I'm sure I look maniacal.

He says, "You better get up, Deputy Hough. I'm not sure your dogs would let me help you."

I chuckle breathlessly. "Remus, jump. Harry, jump." I raise a hand as my dogs lay down.

The sheriff helps me to my feet. A Deputy's car pulls up. I get in, and the sheriff lets the dogs into the back seat.

❦

I GET BACK TO THE HOUSE AWASH IN A FLURRY OF ACTIVITY. I THANK Deputy Morgan for the lift. He grins at me and says, "I'll see you Monday morning, Deputy."

"No way in hell," I mutter, and he laughs. I let the dogs out, and they bolt to the big sandbox by the trash barrel that I created for a dog toilet. I respond louder, "Thanks, Morgan. Stay healthy."

He waves and slowly drives out the driveway, maneuvering around vehicles and crime scene investigators.

The backdoor has been covered with a sheet of plywood, so I detour around the corpse through the garage. I notice the opossum isn't around. I look behind the recycle barrel to find him looking up at me. I tell him, "Good job, buddy. Make sure you leave some food for the dogs. You know how Muffy gets."

I enter the kitchen from the garage. Denise runs up and throws her arms around me. I close my eyes and hold her close. She sobs, "I was so worried."

"I know, Love," I murmur. "Needed to be done. It's over now. Those that survived are in custody. Could have been worse."

Denise kisses me passionately as I hear a pair of feet approach quickly and another pair of arms wrap around us. I pull Aliyah into our hug as I open my eyes.

Denise murmurs, "My family is whole again." Aliyah kisses my lips quickly and burrows into our group hug.

"So, are we staying here tonight?" I ask. "I need a shower and a bed"

"Agent Howell said it would take most of the morning to process everything," Denise says. "It's four o'clock now. They are currently processing Aliyah's room."

"They allowed me to get some clothes," Aliyah says. "My parents would host us, but getting there in our current state might be problematic."

"The loveseat in my office is a pull-out, Aliyah. We could let you sleep there," I say.

Aliyah and Denise share a look that I can't manage to comprehend in my current state. Aliyah smiles at me. "Okay, Marc."

Agent Howell walks up with a short, "Kph."

We release each other to face him. He says, "We need your shotgun for evidence. You will get it back eventually."

I slide the weapon off my shoulder, clear it, and hand it over. He takes it to the table and puts it in a big bag. I don't volunteer my Glock. He fills out a slip and hands it to me. "Your receipt," he says.

"Thanks," is all I can manage.

Denise says, "I have one for the Shockwave, my M4, and Aliyah's Ruger."

I nod. Agent Howell says in passing, "Good job apprehending Michael and Seamus Connolly."

"Thanks," I mutter with a grimace.

"He thinks you're a cowboy," Denise says. "He has to send resources over to the Connolly trailer."

Howell gives her a reptilian gaze. I warn, "Agent Howell, do not mess with my fiancé." He looks at me sternly. I tell him, "Why don't you tell us when we can get some sleep."

He nods. "We finished processing your master suite. It didn't take long since nothing relative to the investigation happened there. We'll want to get some pictures in the daylight, but we can get those once you're awake again. We'll probably be here until about noon. We're going to be in Miss Sadduzai's room for a while. We didn't start it until after you left, and Ms. Schneider asked us to make it a priority. It will take a while since there was a death there."

"Miss Sadduzai can sleep on the pull-out in my office," I tell him. "If we can use our bedroom, I'm going to shower. Help yourself to the coffee machine. Grounds are in the can next to the can opener. Goodnight."

Denise and Aliyah set up the pull-out bed in my office while I start to disrobe. I put the Glock in the gunsafe and hang the tac vest in the closet next to Denise's. I pull off the body armor and walk down the hall to give it to one of the investigators. She bags it, logs it, and hands me a receipt. I doubt I'll get the body armor back. Too bad, it might come in handy the way my life has been going.

I stop by to check on Buster. He raises his head as I approach. It looks like he was patched up already. "Come to the bedroom, Buster."

He gets up, and I carry his dog bed to the bedroom. I manage to get it tucked into the corner without it being in Denise's path to the bathroom.

I return to the bedroom and strip off. I crawl into the shower and scrub down vigorously. I can feel the left shoulder complain as I scrub my hair. I probably wasn't supposed to get the dressing wet, but I just can't manage to care.

I dry off and brush my teeth. When I finish, I lean on the counter and look at the guy in the mirror. He looks a lot rougher than I anticipated. We inspect each other. He doesn't look disappointed in what he sees.

I point a finger at him. "Don't go getting all maudlin. You did kill again, but it was a bunch of bad guys trying to hurt the people you love. You avoided killing the ones that you could, and the ones you killed were righteous. All life is precious, but you didn't have a choice. It's a good thing you survived."

He nods gently back to me. We wave at each other, and I go to get some pajama shorts. I stop short as I see the two beautiful ladies in my household standing naked in the process of dressing for bed. They murmur quietly to each other, so I ignore them and pull on the shorts.

I see a glass of water at my bedside. I take a big sip and ensure my M&P is in place in the nightstand before I crawl in bed.

Aliyah stands beside Denise - Denise in her poet's shirt and Aliyah in her nearly transparent cotton gown. Aliyah says, "Marc, there is glass on the floor of your office."

"I'll vacuum it up real quick. Give me a minute," I tell her. I steel myself to climb off the heavenly mattress.

Denise looks concerned. She shares a look with Aliyah. Eventually, Aliyah says, "Marc, I don't want to sleep alone tonight."

I raise my head to take in her sexy silhouette. "Then don't, Aliyah. We have plenty of room, and if you want it, you can have four arms wrapped around you to keep you safe."

She smiles shyly and blushes, but Denise's smile is brilliant as she winks at me.

Aliyah says, "I would like that."

"Then get in here, Pet," I respond without thinking.

Denise laughs as Aliyah looks shocked. Denise says, "You will probably get a bye for tonight, but a lot of amazing sexual pleasure comes with being Marc's pet, Allie. Prepare yourself."

Aliyah launches across the bed to devour my mouth. I pull her to me, and Aliyah grinds her crotch into my hip as I squeeze her petite ass. She moans and throws a leg over my thigh as Denise slides into the bed and turns the light out.

Aliyah finally releases my mouth. I look at Denise. "Are you okay with this?"

Denise nods energetically. "Yes. I want you to make love to me while I make love to Allie. I want to watch you make love to Allie. You

two are the people I love most in life. Having you both as loving partners is more than I could have ever dreamed."

Aliyah says, "I will need to learn a lot. I am completely lost in the
bedroom. As much as I love Denise, my uncertainty makes it awkward.
There's so much we haven't tried."

"Allie?" She quickly deduces that I'm trying on her nickname and
nods. "Allie, there is plenty of time for us to learn," I say. "This is new
territory for me, too. But if we love each other and are patient - and
discrete - we can make this work. Now get some sleep, Allie."

"Yes, Sir," she says and drapes an arm over my chest and lays her
head on my shoulder.

Denise leans over Aliyah and kisses me. As we part, she says, "Marc
you are the love of my life - the dream I never thought I would experience. I never thought my love for Allie would grow into this, but I
desire her too. Thank you for being you. I love you so much."

"I love you too, Denise," I tell her and kiss her again.

Aliyah murmurs into my neck. "I love you both so much. I do not
know what to do with all this emotion."

"Sleep on it, Allie, my love," I tell her and turn off my bedside light.

Denise lies on top of Aliyah and I wrap an arm around them both.
I squeeze them gently as I offer a short prayer of thanks for being able
to protect my Denise and my Aliyah and surviving the effort. After I
send a mental 'amen' to whoever our divine parent is, I slowly fade into
unconsciousness.

⚜

I SLOWLY WAKE TO POUNDING OUTSIDE THE HOUSE. I'M CURLED
around Aliyah's petite form, and she is curled up with her face between
Denise's breasts. My right hand is resting on Denise's hip, and her
hand is resting on mine. Her other hand is curled beneath Aliyah's
head as though she is holding the young woman's face to her
décolletage.

Denise groans at the noise. I check the time - 7:45 in the morning.
'*Well, shit!*'

I get up slowly and look out Denise's window. I see someone

standing in the yard in front of my office's south window. I think that's where Denise was when she shot the two attackers. I open the window and call out. "What do you think you're doing?"

The slightly rotund man with a Dekalb seed cap and coveralls has a cheesy little mustache. He startles to see me, my pistol resting on the window sill.

"We're securing the exterior. We have a contract, and we have to finish within fifteen minutes per compromised window or door," he says with an air of self-importance.

I tell him, "Well, I'm the homeowner. I'm also of the opinion that you should be asking my permission to start hammering on my house despite the fact that the work obviously needs doing. I've had people shooting at me all night, and now I am trying desperately to get some sleep. That makes me very cranky."

"Uh...the Agent in Charge called and told us to take care of it," he says.

"No problem. I'll go have a word with him. How many more do you have to do?" I ask as pleasantly as possible.

"Two windows on the west side, we already redid the door." He seems quite pleased with himself.

"Absolutely freaking fantastic," I mutter as I try to close the window quietly.

I turn to the ladies, both of who are looking up at me bleary-eyed. "Go back to sleep, my lovelies. Don't explain sleeping arrangements until you talk to me. I'm going to do my best to not beat the shit out of a KBI agent."

I get dressed in jeans, t-shirt, and a quarter-zip sweatshirt. I figure with all the debris in the house, I better put on my boots. I grab ropers instead of hiking boots, clip my M&P onto the back of my waistband, and leave the bedroom as quietly as I can.

I walk into the kitchen to find three investigators sitting at my dining table - a geeky young Asian man with coke-bottle glasses, a homely brunette young lady with acne scars, and a middle-aged guy with dirty blond hair who looks like a professor, complete with a tweed jacket and pipe. Luckily the pipe isn't lit. "Moving in, folks?"

The geeky young man said, "The AC said we could have coffee."

"I agreed to you having coffee. I didn't agree to you all moving in. The AIC is Howell?" I ask.

The geek says, "We say 'AC,' now. And yes, Howell is the AC."

"Get out of my house, you little prick," I bark. "Drain your coffee and leave."

Suddenly there is a very pissed off Rottweiler standing next to the guy, growling. Three more huge dogs bolt through the massive dog door to back up their injured buddy.

The two kids get up and bolt. The older guy moves slower as he takes in the dogs.

He asks "Are the taller ones hybrids?"

I sigh, "Yeah. Great Dane and Bull Mastiff. The breeder was trying to breed a superior guard-attack dog. He named them after dogs in some stories by his favorite author - calls them 'Cuon.' I've read the books, but my imagination didn't look anything like these two when I read the description. Regardless, they're great dogs. The Mastiff and Rottweiler are great breeds, too. I've been very pleased with all four of them.

The guy nods sagely.

"Do I need to charge you rent?" I ask.

"Huh? Uh, no. Thank you for the talk," he says and leaves quickly.

I look at Buster, "Go to bed." I point to the bedroom, and he marches back to his bed with a whimper.

I head outside to find Agent Howell. The geeky kid is haranguing Agent Howell. Howell finally gets fed up with him. "Investigator Kim! That man..." Howell points to me "...killed ten criminals and shot another five last night because they threatened his family. His would be the last house in the whole fucking country I would choose to squat in."

The geeky kid starts, "But, sir!"

Howell holds his finger up to forestall the kid from talking and pulls out his phone. In two strokes of his fingers, Howell is calling someone on his cell phone as I walk up.

Agent Howell says, "Hey Tristan, Simon here. Investigator Kim has become a liability...Yeah, I know he's young, but that's no excuse for a lack of professionalism. I will be writing him up...Look, Tristan. I've got another three hours of work to do for four investigators, I only have three investigators. One of them is the slowest guy in the lab, and then Kim is pissing off the VICTIM. Nessa is the only one pulling her weight...huh?...yeah, that victim...what?..." Howell's face takes on an evil grin. "Sure, Tristan. Standby..."

Howell turns on his speakerphone and says, "Go ahead, Tristan."

A gravelly voice yells out of the speaker. "Kim! Are you there?"

The geeky kid gulps and says, "Yes, sir."

"Good," the guy on the phone responds. Suddenly his voice doubles in volume. "ARE YOU OUT OF YOUR EVER-LOVING MIND? We do NOT ANTIGONIZE THE FUCKING VICTIMS! AM I CLEAR?

"Yes, sir!" the geeky kid gasps.

"GOOD!," the voice yells. "I need Ben at this site, so you better be taking up the slack! You like to tell me how you have great leadership potential. Boy, I don't ever want to hear those words out of your mouth. You want to convince me? Show me! Move! Get to work!"

"Yes, sir," the kid mutters. I almost feel sorry for him.

Agent Howell, "Ask Mr. Hough if you can finish inside. They didn't get much sleep, so some of them might still need to sleep. And don't upset his dogs. They will eat you."

I chuckle and decide to build the kid up a bit. "Investigator Kim, let me check on the ladies. I'll feed the dogs on the way in and let you know when we're ready."

Investigator Kim says, "We still need to plot the crime scene. It's light enough now, and we should have started already. Starting a shift in the middle of the night is tough."

I nod, "Yes it is. Short breaks are key. You can rotate your team, and it will keep the work moving while allowing everyone to get a little break." He looks at me funny. I tell him, "I learned that as a sergeant in the army."

Kim says, "Oh! That makes sense."

Agent Howell says dryly, "Sounds like you got everything in hand now, Investigator Kim."

Investigator Kim says bashfully, "Yes, sir. If you see anything we missed, please let me know."

I turn away to go do my part. Agent Howell calls out, "Mr. Hough, I got statements from Ms. Schneider and Miss Sadduzai last night, but I still need to get one from you."

"Come along, Agent Howell," I tell him.

I stop in the garage to feed and water the dogs. I look behind the recycle barrel to see my little marsupial friend sleeping. I point at the animal, and Agent Howell takes a look.

"Let it be," I say as he reaches for his firearm. "It's not rabid. I'll chase it out when I get a better dog door."

Howell says, "One of our agents swears 'possum stew is a taste of heaven."

I grab Buster's bowl and say, "I wouldn't know," I usher Howell inside and have him take a seat at the dining table.

I take Buster his food bowl. Denise is lying in the middle of the bed, and Aliyah is on Denise's left. I nod. Denise opens her eyes and smiles at me. She says, "I guess it's time to get up."

"Take your time, but yes. They need to process my office. They may think Aliyah is still in there."

Denise says, "No problem. The glass made it unsafe, so we all squeezed into our bed."

Aliyah says with a yawn, "That is what happened. We do not need to mention how I was poked in the bum all night long by someone's hard cock." She blushes furiously when she realizes what she just said.

We chuckle. I crawl on the bed to kiss Denise languidly and caress her breasts. I release her, and she whimpers prettily. I explain, "I gotta go, Love. Agent Howell needs to take my statement."

She pouts teasingly, "But that promised to be such a nice wakeup."

"I'll make it up to you," I tell her before brushing another kiss on her lips.

Aliyah gets up to meet me at the end of the bed. She blushes prettily in her provocative nightdress before stepping in for a tight hug. She relaxes her grip and looks up at me questioningly. I kiss her lips gently, and she opens her lips to welcome me. I caress her back and release her. "More to follow," I say to reassure her. She smiles shyly at me before looking over at Denise.

Denise opens her arms, and Aliyah crawls into bed to hug her.

Denise murmurs, "We will figure it out, Allie. Be patient and trust that we love you."

I blow them both a kiss and wave to Buster before returning to Agent Howell.

I pick up the cups off the table, wash them, and make a fresh pot of coffee as I start telling my story. I start with the two guys in the pickup the night Clan Connolly broke Joseph out of jail in Lyndon and finish with me blacking out sometime after I found Joseph Connolly.

By the time my story is finished, the coffee is ready, and Denise is wrapped around my shoulders, kissing my head, and squeezing me tight. Aliyah is sitting at the table wrapped in a throw from the sofa over her jeans and sweatshirt.

Howell asks me a couple of questions for clarification before closing his notebook. He thanks us all, and heads outside.

13

AFTERMATH

The ladies and I work together to make a brunch of French Toast, Sausage, and eggs. I don't have any non-pork sausage that Aliyah can eat. However, I do have some ground turkey, old bread, and an extra egg. Denise whips up the batter for the French Toast. Aliyah seasons eggs, and I mix up the turkey into small sausage patties.

The female investigator runs in and begs, "May I use the bathroom please?"

Aliyah says, "Sure. This way." She leads the investigator to the guest bath and returns to find Denise and I hogging the stove with the sausage and French Toast. She reports, "She's going to process your office as soon as she is done."

"Good," I respond. "The sooner they're out of here, the sooner we can start cleaning up."

Denise finishes the French Toast, so Aliyah starts the scrambled eggs. She finishes the eggs and plates the slightly moist eggs. "Perfect!" I exclaim as I slide sausage patties onto the plates. We sit down and stuff ourselves on the stack of french toast with butter and preserves, butter and syrup, or bananas and Nutella. Not a crumb survives, and the coffee pot is empty.

Aliyah calls her parents and talks to them for about twenty minutes about everything that happened last night. During that call, I send last night's video from my phone - the 'bodycam' footage - to Sheriff Eskola. Then I help Denise clean up the kitchen. When Aliya gets off the phone, she says her parents offered to let us stay with them while home repairs are underway.

"I don't know how long before we have this cleaned up," I tell her. "I won't want to impose for long. Plus, we have the dogs."

Aliyah says, "No problem. Bring the dogs. They said however long we need."

So, we hurry to clean up the kitchen before we pack bags, electronics, weapons, and dogs into both vehicles. Denise drives Aliyah to her parents' house with Harry, Muffy, and Remus. I follow in the pickup with Buster and the truck bed filled with dog beds, a bunch of suitcases, a large bag of dog food, and dog bowls.

We arrive at the Sadduzai house, and I carry the bags in. Liyana sets Denise and me up in a mother-in-law suite that I didn't know they had - essentially a two bedroom suite. I get a call from Sheriff Eskola just as I set the bags into the room.

Aliyah leads Denise and me back to the kitchen while I talk.

"Hello, Sheriff. How can I help you?" I answer.

"Deputy Hough! I need you."

"A little more specific, Sheriff," I tell him.

"I need a report from you of what happened at the trailer park and what happened to Deputy Crowley," he says. *"Plus I have seven injured patrol deputies on medical leave, plus another four corrections deputies. I have three dead patrol deputies, one dead corrections deputy, and two dead dispatchers. I need help, Deputy Hough."*

"Sheriff, I have no intention of working in law enforcement ever again," I tell him.

"You were deputized for twenty-four hours. Time's not up yet," he says. *"Seriously, Mr. Hough. I need the help. Actually, I need help for six weeks until some of the injured recover, and I can hire two new dispatchers and four new deputies. I might be able to put you back on reserve status earlier depending on how fast folks come back from injuries and the speed of hiring. What do you say, Mr. Hough?"*

"I need to discuss it with Denise. Gimme a minute," I tell him.

Denise looks at me expectantly as I mute the phone. I tell her, "Sheriff Eskola wants me to be a deputy for six weeks. He has eleven wounded deputies, four dead deputies, and two dead dispatchers. He needs the help."

Denise looks at me expectantly. "So what do you want to do?"

"I want to say no," I tell her.

"So why haven't you?" she asks.

I sigh heavily. "They were there when we needed help. What if someone else needs help, and there's no one there?"

Denise gives me a grin. "Sounds like you know what to do," she says.

"Smartass," I tell her.

She glides in closely and kisses me. "Whose smartass?"

"Mine," I agree. I squeeze her tightly, and she lays her head on my shoulder. I pick up the phone and say, "Okay, Sheriff. I can be there in a little over an hour. I'm in North Topeka right now."

I spend a few minutes trying to get the dogs situated. It becomes apparent quickly, that this isn't going to work for them. Large beasts with wagging tails don't work well in houses that aren't prepared for them. Liyana and Muhaimin's house is not prepared.

Denise shoos me off to 'work' saying, "Aliyah and I will figure the dogs out. Worst case, we can take Harry, Muffy, and Remus back to the farm. We need to keep an eye on Buster for a bit, and his vet is in west Topeka. Take Remus with you. Go. Be safe. I love you."

I smile and tell her, "I love you, too." I check to ensure I still have the badge and my pistols. Liyana hands me a full travel mug of coffee, and Remus and I hop in the truck and journey down to Lyndon.

◈

I ASSUMED THAT THE SHERIFF'S OFFICE WAS AT THE COURTHOUSE, BUT I arrived there and discovered my error. I pulled my phone, Googled the address, and backtracked to the veterinary clinic. I turned west and finally arrived at the Sheriff's Office. It's a bigger building than I anticipated for such a rural community. Then again, I had assumed they only had four-to-five deputies. I should have known better after the sheriff's run-down of last night's events - not a good record on my assumptions.

The sheriff immediately put me to work documenting my account of what happened at the trailer park last night. He gave me a Sheriff's Deputy windbreaker with a matching ball cap and account credentials to their system, so I started writing. Remus lay on the floor next to me at the desk.

The sheriff reviewed my document and asked me some questions, which I answered by editing the document. He also showed me where my video was stored on the department's servers, so I copied my document into the official system and added a reference to that file in the record and submitted it as an official report.

Despite the sheriff saying he would get my account of events from Agent Howell, he asked me to write that up as well in a Word document. After I completed that and gave it to the sheriff, he gave me the tour. He introduced me to the Under-Sheriff, the deputies present and the service staff for the jail. He told me that I need to be prepared for anything, but that I would likely be manning the office unless a tactical situation arises. It has become readily apparent that I'm the sheriff's designated point man.

Once the tour was complete, the sheriff assigned me a bunch of online training materials to review and had me start with Kansas and county regulations on search-and-seizure, *etcetera*. It was boring, but since he wants me to serve as more than an executioner, I need to know it. It was very similar to what I learned in the army. I did that for about two hours before the sheriff sent me home with instructions to finish as much of the online training as possible tomorrow from home and pick up uniforms in Topeka first thing Monday morning. He also told me to keep bringing Remus with me - his K-9 deputy and dog were both among the dead. Remus and I will likely be the interim K-9 unit until they hire a replacement deputy and find a dog.

I texted Denise that I was heading home as I took Remus for a quick walk. Her response befuddled me. *'Meet me at the farm! :D'*

I sent an acknowledgement, loaded Remus in the truck, and started the twenty minute drive home with just a short detour for gas. I called Dad on the way home. Gretchen answered the phone.

After I announced myself, she gasped. "Oh, thank God! Marcus, I was so worried! Are you and Denise okay? I heard both of you were shot."

"Uh, yeah Gretchen. We're okay," I tell her. "Denise took a round through her leg muscle, and I had a graze across my shoulder. We're both okay. How did you find out about that?"

"Sherry Morgan's son is a deputy. He's been staying with her until he goes back to work. He was involved in something last night, and he heard about it."

"Fortunately, we were able to keep him out of the shit," I tell her. "I can't tell you any more about it."

She exclaims, "Oh!" Then she quietly says, "Carl is asleep." She gets a little louder. "Mr. Hough...er..." softer again "Marc, I was so worried about the two of you."

'Hmm. Marc. Not Marcus. Interesting.'

"We're both okay, Gretchen," I ensure her. "We're both managing with ibuprofen for the pain. Denise is walking without a limp, and I can use my arm with only minor twinges. As a matter of fact, the sheriff deputized me, so I'm my way home from my first half-day as a deputy."

"Damnit, Marc! You don't need to be putting yourself in danger!" she scolds. I chew on that for a minute while chuckling at her scolding. "It's not funny, Marc!"

"Gretchen, calm down," I scold her in return. "There's no need for you to worry."

"Okay," she says quietly. "I don't want to think about you or Denise being hurt."

"I understand," I tell her. "I wouldn't want you to be hurt in any way, either. You are too giving and too sweet to suffer." I change gears. "Please tell Dad that I'm okay, and that Denise and I will come visit tomorrow. Plan for us to join him for lunch."

"Will the Muslim girl come, too?" she asks.

"I don't know. I need to check in with Denise. She's been holding down the home front while I've been in-processing at the Sheriff's Office today," I tell her. "Let's assume Aliyah will be with us. If I find out differently, I will let you know."

"Okay," she says. "Bye, Marc," she says dreamily.

I think, '*Strange.*' I tell her, "Goodbye, Gretchen. Stay safe, and be well."

I get to the farm and initially I think no one is there. Harry and Muffy run out to greet me, and I see Denise's SUV parked in front of her garage slot. Both garage doors are open.

I back the truck into my garage bay. I get out of the truck, grabbing the small pad I used for notes at the office. I walk around the truck and let Remus out. He runs toward the machine shed. That's when I notice a large RV parked on the other side of Denise's POD. It looks like a big taupe and brown tourist bus. It's barely visible from the west.

I walk closer and note an electric drop cord running into the machine shed. "Hello? Denise?"

I notice the vehicle is jacked and chock-blocked in place. There is an extension sticking out behind the POD. I hear her call out, "In the back, Marc!"

"Okay!" I holler. I enter the RV and notice there is another extension out the other side. It makes the living space about the size of a single-wide trailer house.

Denise emerges from the back, and closes the door. "Hello, my Love," she greets me. She is wearing midnight blue yoga pants, black flats, and a waist-length raw silk sweater as she bounces towards me. Her full breasts bounce slightly as she closes with me. I lose myself in her embrace and warm, moist lips. I squeeze her firm tushy to elicit a moan that she releases into my mouth.

"I love you, Denise," I tell her.

"Oh yes, Marc, my Love, my husband. I love you and have missed you today. I wanted so badly to be with you. I think we need to have some quality time," she says with a sultry gaze.

"Husband, huh?" I respond. "I'm in; although, I thought I'd only earned 'fiancé,' Love."

"Legally you are correct, Marc." She grabs my hand and holds it between her breasts. "However, I'm married to you here."

"Me too, Denise," I agree. "I would drag you outside for some celebratory sex, but it's pretty chilly out."

She wraps her arms around me. "That would be fabulous, but you're right - it's too cold for me without a fire. Too bad! Rory came by earlier; it would probably be safe for the rest of the day. Anyway, Rory said that apparently your neighbor to the south wants to sell their land. She heard about all of our issues and the raid at the trailer park. She has decided it's too dangerous and wants to move to Topeka. Rory left her contact information in case you're interested."

I tuck that tidbit away for later, "Where did you get the RV?" I wave my hand at the walls of the house on wheels.

"Oh! It belongs to Liyana and Muhaimin," Denise explains. "They take an extended road trip every year, and Muhaimin likes to sleep in his own bed when they travel. Apparently, he thought this was a worthwhile investment. Liyana said it's amazing considering how he can pinch a penny in half for any other expense. They came and set it up as a 'thank you' for protecting Aliyah. After Muhaimin got it all set up, Aliyah took them home."

"Okay," I reply. "Uh, how's the bed in here?"

"Pretty big and firm," she says with a grin. "Shall we give it a test drive? I just finished putting sheets on it."

"Lets," I say before giving her a wet kiss and picking her up by her ass.

The smart, funny, composed, beautiful woman that is my fiancé squeals with delight. We squeeze through the narrow door and collapse onto the mattress. It feels like a futon on a wooden platform. There's just barely enough room for my feet to shuffle on either side of the bed.

Denise pulls her sweater over her head as she kicks off her shoes while I take off my boots. She pushes off her yoga pants and panty in one deft move as I strip out of my clothes. Once I'm naked, I see that Denise is leaning on the pillows with her knees splayed, fingers rubbing her own moisture over her labia and clit while looking at me hungrily.

I crawl between her knees and claim a kiss, suckle on each of her breasts momentarily, and then drop between her thighs to sample her nectar. I use my mouth and fingers on Denise's pussy to bring her to an orgasm. I don't have the patience for more. I need her now!

I shuffle forward and enter her quivering quim, pushing inexorably deeper to the accompaniment of Denise's gasps of encouragement. We both reach our releases quickly and quite loudly. Rather than collapsing on top of Denise, I roll off to the side and pull her onto my chest.

Denise murmurs, "Hmmm. That was awesome."

I chuckle, "It's a good start, Love."

Denise crawls over the top of me and leans low. She sways side to side, dragging her distended nipples across my chest. She murmurs, "I wonder what I can do to facilitate getting round two started."

"I think you may be onto something," I tell her. Denise smiles brightly, and I start a nearly magical recovery. "You know...," I muse. "...if you were to do that while looking south, I could pleasure you while you tease me."

"Mmmm," she says before leaning down to devour my mouth for a minute or three. I'm starting to feel pretty good about the progress down south. Denise bites her lip as she crawls off me before mounting me again with her succulent labia right above my face.

I reach up for a lick of Denise's delights. A short moment later, my half-erect member is consumed by her hot mouth. I bring Denise off three more times with my mouth and fingers before she crawls off my face and mounts up cowgirl.

I sit up and start suckling her lovely, full breasts as she bounces on my cock. We roll to the side, and I pound her hard from the missionary mount. After Denise comes hard, I pull out and roll her onto her hands and knees before mounting her from behind. I pull her hands behind her back and pin them with one hand while I fuck her hot spasming pussy.

Denise's ridged muscles clasp me hard as a strong orgasm takes her, screaming and gasping her bliss. The stimulation is too much for me. I unload inside her, continuing to thrust erratically. Denise's orgasm spirals higher, and she starts squirting around my pounding cock with a loud shriek.

I stay inside Denise to feel her aftershocks squeezing delightfully. I release her hands and she rolls to her side. I lay down next to her. She crawls onto my chest. I pull the comforter over the top of us to keep off the chill.

"Mmmm. I'm loving the cuddles," she says. "I can't believe how much I missed you today. I was acting the role of the wife of the household, and I would have liked to have you beside me."

"So, how did this whole RV thing come about?" I ask.

"Well, Liyana told me quietly that Muhaimin's expectations were that you and I would sleep in separate beds in the house since we are not legally married," she explains. "I told her that I need to make love to you at least once every day, and that separate sleeping arrangements wouldn't work for us."

"I agree."

Denise continues as she plays with my hair. "I told her I would find a hotel. That's when she offered this. She said they really only use it about once per year, but that Muhaimin spends a full day on it each month keeping it ready. It runs on diesel fuel, so for the size it's fairly economical to run. Using our own power and water from our hose, we just need to take it out once each week to empty the sewage. Muhaimin said theoretically we could run it into our lagoon, but there's also a KOA campground in south Topeka that has the facilities to pump it out. I think he liked that option better because it would give the engine a little exercise."

"Okay," I agree. "We'll get a schedule set up. It's probably best that we stay in the county since I'm a deputy for the moment."

"True," Denise says. "Fortunately, it's less restrictive for me since I work for the state court system." She starts stroking my thigh. "We can still use the kitchen in the house, so we don't mess this one up. Actually, unless we have contractors on site, we could use the bathrooms over there, too. We can keep these for emergency use only."

I shrug and say, "Still need to keep everything clean, but yeah. Definitely."

Denise strokes my cock gently, and things start to look up. She says distractedly, "Liyana said that Muhaimin thinks we'll be using the spare beds in the sitting and dining areas. She smirked when she said it." I hum in acknowledgement. She continues, "She also said that he is certain that Aliyah will be sleeping there when she comes to visit. She looked at me rather pointedly. I told her that Aliyah is my dear friend, and that I would support her in whatever she decides. Liyana had this weird, secretive smile on her lips."

I ask, "Um...did you hear that?" I roll out of bed carefully, and pull my Glock from its holster.

Denise follows my lead. She says, "I didn't hear the dogs."

"I thought I heard a car door," I say just before a knock sounds on the door to the RV.

"Who is it?" I ask just before the door opens. I raise my weapon and prepare to deal with intruders.

"Hello-o!" sounds from the front of the bus. "Denise? Marc? It's me!"

Denise calls out, "Good grief, Allie! You scared the shit out of us! We're in the back."

I see a blue-patterned scarf wrapped around her head as a hijab. She steps in, closes the door, and fiddles with it.

Aliyah smiles brightly and says, "If you two are going to engage in bedroom acrobatics, you might want to lock the door."

I hang our clothes from hooks and set my pistol on the floor next to the bed. I sit on the mattress and lean against the pillows. Denise rests her head on my shoulder as we watch Aliyah walk back to us. She has very high-heeled stiletto shoes and a black trenchcoat on.

Aliyah leans against the doorjamb. She surveys our naked bodies and bites her lip. Finally, she gathers either her thoughts or her courage.

Aliyah says, "Denise, you have been my best friend for many years. You may not know that I have desired you for my lover nearly as long as I've known you. I want to know the pleasure of making love to you." Her gaze is searing as she takes in Denise's slow nod and naked body.

Aliyah turns to me, "Marc, I was so jealous of you when Denise told me about you. I couldn't convince myself to pursue Denise despite my desire for her. You came and took the opportunity away. I think you knew this immediately when I met you in the hospital." I nod, and she continues. "I was molested in middle school by my favorite teacher. He pinned me to the wall and pierced my vagina with his finger. He broke my hymen, and it hurt not only my body but my soul. I trusted him. Since then I've had difficulty with any touch from a man - even my own father and brothers. Then I met you. You make me feel safe. You make me feel beautiful. You make me feel sexually desired, but also treasured. I love being held by you. I love being with you."

She bites her lip, so I nod to encourage her. Aliyah says, "I don't know you well yet, but I plan to. I would like to explore the pleasures and intimacy that you share with Denise. Sometimes together with Denise, but I think I might also like to try it on my own too after a while - if the two of you will permit it."

Aliyah steps forward off the door jamb into the small bedroom. Denise and I look at each other. She nods. I nod back to her. We clasp hands and turn our attention back to Aliyah. Denise nods to Aliyah.

Aliyah bites her lip and unwinds her hijab. Her glorious, lustrous dark hair cascades down past her shoulders to rest at the top of her pert breasts. She starts to untie the belt around her trench coat as she says, "Since this is your new, temporary home, I thought I would bring you a house warming present..."

Aliyah opens the coat and shrugs it off her shoulders to reveal herself - standing in her heels, stockings, a midnight blue garter, and matching balconette brassiere that has the small cups peeled down to reveal her dark areolae and nipples. Her thick bush is dark and lustrous like the hair on her head. Dew drops from her dark, barely visible labia.

"...me."

Denise gets off my shoulder and walks to the foot of the bed on her knees, and I follow, mesmerized by the beautiful woman before us. We step off the bed and wrap her in a group hug. Denise kisses her passionately, as I caress both beauties' bare flesh.

Aliyah turns from Denise's kiss and captures my face in both hands. She looks in my eyes.

Denise says, "Always, Allie."

I nod and add, "Forever, Allie."

The Pakistani beauty devours my mouth and presses her delicious body against mine.

When the kiss breaks, Denise and I each take Aliyah by the hand and guide her to the bed.

As she lays down on the mattress, Aliyah looks up at us both, eyes darting from one to the other. She says, "Please! Make me yours!"

So we do.

End

AFTERWORD

You may recall that I mentioned the first book in this series was a departure from my normal genres. I could have left out the harem element in this one. Aliyah started off as the catalyst for the Connolly family's further misdeeds, but her connection to Denise could not be denied. I was less successful in being concise this time, but still this story is roughly 30% of my full-length novels. I could have thrown in more sex and added a chapter for the claiming of Aliyah, but the story didn't demand it.

I would value your feedback. As you know, Amazon is driven by reviews, so please leave one - especially if you liked it! I love 5-star reviews! Those 5-star reviews are critical because I'll get more exposure to new readers based on the ratings of each book. Plus, it helps to counteract the haters out there. As not all readers will love what I write, it's important to hear from those of you that do, so I can reach a wider audience. As a part-time author, I would appreciate the help. I have at least one more story for Marcus, Denise, and Aliyah in my perverted little mind - probably two. I'm not going to set a threshold of 5-star reviews for them since you all know that I'll write when 1) enough of you bug me about it, or 2) the story develops in mind enough that I have to put it to paper.

I originally was going to call the first book 'My Library Pet,' but landed on 'Surrender' instead since both characters go through a surrender of sorts. Now Aliyah, Denise, and Marcus have all gone through another surrender - giving in to their growing attraction to each other. That transition from a couple to a *ménage à trois* had to be organic. Aliyah's tragic childhood event and her secret desire for Denise set the stage, allowing her to see Marcus from Denise's perspective and growing to love him, too. I think it works. Shoot me a note to let me know what you think.

My wife and I watch Hallmark movies relatively frequently, and I usually end up telling her how the story is going to progress. She usually responds by telling me I should write romance novels. I'm afraid this is about as close to writing romance as I get.

I have a Facebook page and a Patreon site where I publish regular installments of a serial story and other premium content. If you're interested, check out my Patreon site.

Currently I'm working on outlining my space story, my Patreon serial (Master of the Road), and the next Accidental Necromancer (AN4). There is an AN short story on Patreon as a free, public post titled 'Clarice's Admirer.' It has some spoilers in it for the future of the Zombieverse, but if you're jonesing for another installment, it's available until I publish it.

I'm on my FaceBook page 2-3 times each week. I'm a member of several groups, too. Here are a couple I would like to recommend:

- Eden's Lewd Fantasy & Sci-fi Garden. This is Eden Redd's group. Lots of fun to be had, and a lot of the Harem-lit authors hang there. I always make a point to drop in and see

what's going on. Address is https://www.facebook.com/
groups/1582096547490089

- Fantasy/Science/Fiction Cool News and Humor group is
  mostly fans. Good times. Very little in the way of politics.
  Address is a https://www.facebook.com/
  groups/584252842052663/

Amazon won't tell you when my next book lands. The best way to find out is to follow me on my Amazon page or Facebook. Yes, I have done a crap job of keeping my author page up-to-date, but I'm getting better. I'm on Facebook and Patreon more regularly. I've also created a web-site. It's still pretty nascent, but you can find all my books there, and I expect to blog there eventually about my writing and reading.

It's time for me to get back to writing. Watch my FaceBook, Patreon, and Amazon Author Page for updates.

'Til next time.

-JG Jerome
   https://www.facebook.com/JGJeromeAuthor
   https://www.patreon.com/jgjerome
   https://www.jgjerome-author.com
   https://www.amazon.com/JG-Jerome/e/B07TWJJSYL

ABOUT THE AUTHOR

JG Jerome is an emerging author of sci-fi stories. This is JG's ninth book.

JG is a part time author and full-time 'IT Guy.' He grew up a Kansas farm boy, and he describes himself as an old soldier. He lives, works, makes music, and writes in Arizona with his wife.

He dabbles in martial arts, fitness training, cooking, bread baking, photography, drawing, singing, and playing multiple musical instruments. His first book was 'Dumb Luck,' the first book in the three-volume Green Lord series.

In between managing IT projects, he is currently working on a variety of stories in the Zombieverse - the Accidental Necromancer series, and the Master of the Road serial on Patreon.

BOOKS BY JG JEROME

Published On Amazon

the Green Lord series

Dumb Luck

(Book 1)

Welcome to a Green Lord Thanksgiving

(Short Story, Book 1.5)

Courting Crazy

(Book 2)

Dread

(Book 3)

the Accidental Necromancer series

Ghost Story

(Book 1)

Den of Iniquity

(Book 2)

Succubus Rescue

(Book 3)

Published on Patreon

Master of the Road

(published as a serial in multiple posts for Patrons only)

Clarice's Admirer

(Short Story - a single public post)